BEAR HUNTER

Adventures of a
Koyukon Boy

Michael S. Cline

Michael S. Cline (signature)

Glen Erin Press

Glen Erin Press

Homer, Alaska

ISBN 1451563167

EAN-13 9781451563160

Dedication

To the people of Huslia,
may you continue to remember your past
as you prepare for the future.

And to my grandchildren,
Alma, Patrick, Timothy, and those to come,
may you find joy in exploring
and learning to appreciate other cultures.

Acknowledgements

I would like to thank the following people for their help in putting this story together: Patti and Buddy Brown, Mildred Hawkins, and Kelly Cline who read earlier drafts and made helpful suggestions; in Huslia, Franklin and Lillian Simon, the Edwin Simon Family, Steven and Katherine Attla, Richard Derendoff, and Jimmy Huntington who shared their stories and wisdom; and finally, my wife Dotty whose help was invaluable throughout the entire project.

CONTENTS

Introduction vi
Alaska Map viii
Village Picture ix
Chapter 1 – The Hunt 1
Chapter 2 – The Race 20
Chapter 3 – The Potlatch and Dance..................31
Chapter 4 – Beaver Trapping.............................42
Chapter 5 – The Catch 51
Chapter 6 – Going After Caribou......................64
Chapter 7 – The Caribou Hunt 74
Chapter 8 – The Accident..................................85
Chapter 9 – The Hospital 101
Chapter 10 – Muskrat Hunting 112
Chapter 11 – The Sno-go 128
Chapter 12 – The Bear Hunt............................140
Chapter 13 – The Bear Party 151
About the Author...163

Introduction

Set in the mid-1960s this story follows eleven-year-old Simon as he learns to become a Koyukon man in an interior Alaskan Athabascan Indian village like Huslia (hoos'-lia).   It was a time of change, and while many traditional village activities continued as before, some were altered through the use of machines such as outboard boat motors and pickup trucks. Snow machines had just burst on the scene, allowing village hunters and trappers to travel faster and further from the village. While fur parkas, hats, mitts, and caribou skin boots were still chosen to keep warm, other clothing was available at the village store and from catalogs. Families relied on hunting and fishing for meat, but they bought food from the store as well, and these conveniences came at a price—they needed to earn money to pay for them. Most men found jobs out of the village during the summer so they could buy the things their family needed.

Another source of income was racing dogs in other villages and in Fairbanks and Anchorage. Mushers such as Jimmy Huntington, Cue Bifelt, Bergman Sam, And George Attla were winners in these big races and brought fame to the village.

The photographs of activities in the book were taken by the author and provide a picture of what things looked like.

Though the story is about one boy and his family, the characters are compilations of a number of people in the village and the pictures are of several individuals. While I have used names familiar to village people, they are not meant to represent any particular individuals with those names, except in a few cases such as Chief Henry.

There were about 180 residents of the village and 55 children in grades 1 through 8 attended the village school at this time. High school students left the village for boarding school in southeast Alaska, Oregon, or Oklahoma and were gone for 8 months each year. Today the village has its own high school.

Finally, this is a story. I hope that by reading it you will get a feeling of what it was like to be a boy in a village like Huslia at that time and what things were like. Today "Simon" and his friends are raising their own families, but it is a much different world than it was 40 years ago. Perhaps in a small way this story may help in remembering what it was like then.

Michael S. Cline

The village, 1967

CHAPTER 1

THE HUNT

"Simon, get up and make fire."

Simon slowly opened his eyes. It was still dark inside the log cabin but he could make out a faint blue tinge through the window. He rolled over to go back to sleep when he remembered...today was Saturday. Today he was supposed to go look for bears with his father!

Simon threw the covers back and swung his legs over the side of the bed. He winced as his bare feet hit the cold floor. Last night it had been ten below zero outside, and it didn't feel much warmer than that now inside. He shivered as he pulled on his pants over his long underwear. Then came three pairs of socks and his moose hide boots. He struggled into his shirt as he stumbled over to the Yukon stove, opened the door, and began to shove papers, split birch, and a few small pieces of spruce into the large barrel stove. He lit the fire, then kneeled close with the stove door open and held his hands near the fire to warm them. Soon the fire caught on the dry wood and he closed the stove door.

Today was the day! He wished his parents would hurry and get up. Finally he heard their voices so he turned on the light. Simon looked over to see his mother brushing her long black hair and his father reaching for his glasses.

"I'll get more wood in," he called over his shoulder as he pushed the door open and frigid air spilled into the room. He closed the door and called out to the dogs whose heads had lifted at the sound of the door. "You fellas ready to go for a run today?"

As Simon finished splitting and packing in the wood he smelled sourdough hotcakes—his favorite breakfast! He dropped his last armload of wood by the stove and quickly pulled his chair up to the table. He smothered his hotcakes in syrup, then turned to his father, "We'll go out today?"

"I dunno," Edwin replied, "It's pretty cold." Simon's heart sank. He had been waiting for this day for so long. This was to be his first time to look for bears, and now they might not go. Simon imagined his Athabascan Indian ancestors struggling through the snow, spears in hand, searching for bear dens. The cold wouldn't bother them! He could see a young boy—just like him—excitedly hoping to get his first bear and prove he was a Koyukon man. And he could imagine the pride the boy felt when his successful hunt was celebrated at a bear party! Simon awakened from his daydream to ask hopefully, "I'll hook up dogs?"

His father, smiling at Simon's eagerness, said simply, "Go ahead."

Overjoyed, Simon bounded out to the dog yard. He pushed the dogsled he had helped his father make over to where the dogs were tied. He untangled the harnesses, set the hook, then pulled the towline taut and dropped it on the snow. They would take eight dogs. First he would hook up Queenie and Prince, the leaders. Then Ringo and Star, then Blue and the others. Anxious to go, the dogs began barking, howling, and jumping into the air against the chains that held them. They could be heard through the whole village.

Queenie was so anxious that when Simon grabbed her collar and released the tether snap, she nearly knocked him down in her enthusiasm. Though she weighed ninety pounds and stood about three feet high, he was not afraid. He had helped train her since she was a pup. He clutched her collar and they led each other over to the waiting harness. First he shoved her head into the harness, thrust both her front legs into the traces, snapped onto the towline, and she was ready to go. Queenie leaped into the air straining against the harness, her breath puffing fog into the air. The other dogs were just as eager, and it wasn't long before they were hooked up. All the dogs were jumping and barking to be off. By now everyone in the village knew a dog team was ready to go since other village dogs had joined their chorus. They wanted to go too!

Simon ran back into the house to put on more clothes. As he pulled on an extra pair of pants he heard his younger sister, Rosie, ask eagerly, " Can I go with you, Daddy?"

"You know women don't go after bears. It's bad luck. You wouldn't want to give Simon bad luck on his first time would you?"

Rosie hung her head and tugged on one of the shiny black braids that hung over her shoulder. "No, I guess not. But it sure sounds like fun."

Her father replied, "Your mother is going to set some ptarmigan snares across the river. Maybe she'll take you along."

"Can I go with you, Mom?" she asked.

"And me too," Sonja, the youngest, chimed in.

Their mother nodded. "I guess so. You girls can help me make the fences."

"Are you ready, Simon? Do we have everything?" Last night his father had given him the task of getting together the supplies they would need. Simon thought of the things he had tied in the sled: his twenty-two and his dad's 30.06, ammunition for both, a small axe, plenty of rope, matches, tea, sugar, a cooking pot, moose ribs, Pilot Bread crackers, salt, dry fish, and hunting knives.

Simon nodded, "Yeah, everything's there," He and his father walked out to the sled. "You tie everything down good?" his father asked.

"I think so," Simon replied as he tossed a large piece of moose hide with the hair still on it to sit on in the sled.

Edwin leaned over and tugged the rope that tied the rolled canvas bundle to the slats of the sled. "Did you bring the dog chains?"

"Uh…no, but I'll get 'em." Simon rushed over to the cache and pulled out the short chains used for tying the dogs when the team was stopped.

"Here they are."

"Put them in this bag. You ready now?

"Uh huh."

Edwin removed the heavy fishhook shaped steel hook from its hole in the ground where it had been holding the sled and dogs back, and Simon scrambled onto the already moving sled. They were off!

Although it was nine o'clock when they left, the sky was still a dark blue. The stars had disappeared and a few spears of sunlight were beginning to show on the southeastern horizon between the trees and hills. Simon's father rode on the runners on the back of the sled, urging the dogs on and grunting to them either, "Gee," or "Haw," when the trail forked. The bump of the sled, the hiss of the snow on the runners, and the dogs' panting was all that could be heard.

Simon gripped the side of the sled. He could just see Gil and Gary's faces when they heard he got his first bear. Would it be a big one? He hoped so! Then he squeezed his eyes shut. If I think like that it could bring me bad luck.

Just then the dogs started behaving strangely. They had their noses in the air and the hair on their backs was standing up. Although he strained to see from his sitting position, Simon couldn't see anything. "What do the dogs smell, Dad?"

Edwin leaned over the sled's handlebars and said quietly, "Moose. There's three over there."

At that instant the dogs saw the moose too, and veered off the trail towards them. Edwin jammed his foot down hard on the brake, and dirt and snow sprayed out, but the sled barely slowed.

"Quick! Give me the hook!"

Simon reached down, grabbed the hook from its place on the sled, and handed it to his father.

"Get ready for a quick stop!" Edwin warned.

As they closed on the moose, Edwin reached out and hooked a birch tree. Snap! They weren't moving anymore. The moose were standing still, not fifty feet away.

"Good thing I made that hook line out of braided nylon," Edwin whispered.

The dogs bristled and barked at the moose that had squared around to face the oncoming team. Although they looked big and awkward, they were anything but that. Simon knew these animals could cripple or kill a dog with one well-placed kick.

"We'll shoot one?" Simon asked hopefully.

"No, we already got one in the cache."

Those few words spooked the moose and they turned and disappeared into the trees.

Edwin pulled the hook off the tree and guided the team back to the trail. Once they were on their way again, Simon asked, "Where will we look for bears?"

"Down below our fish camp where those two old bear dens are, not far from where we hunted last year. That's where I got my first bear."

Simon knew his grandfather had shown the dens to his father when he was young. Now it was his turn. He was both excited and a little scared. He imagined his dad and grandfather searching for a bear den on a day just like this. Did they find a bear the first time? Had his dad been scared? What would it feel like to really shoot a bear?

The country became more familiar as they came to the river. Just at the next bend their fish camp came into view. Simon saw the fish-drying racks and the tent frame poles waiting for next summer. But now they went beyond the fish camp to a small birch-covered hill. As they approached the area, Simon looked around. The trees were different here. Instead of the spruce thickets on the higher ground or the willows and alders near the lakes or rivers, white birch was the main growth on this small, sandy hill. He'd need to remember this place.

Edwin stopped the team and Simon jumped out and began to unhitch and chain the dogs to small trees.

"There's a den on the right side of the hill about halfway up," Edwin said as he began loosening the tarp holding the supplies. He handed Simon the twenty-two and put the other supplies in the small pack that Simon put on his back. With his rifle in one hand and the small ax in the other, Edwin led the way. Simon carried the twenty-two in case they should surprise a flock of ptarmigan or a grouse. Even though he was used to being in the woods, Simon had to struggle to keep up since his father moved quickly. Somehow he seemed to know how to pick the best way through the brush. At a nod from his father Simon separated from him. Keeping within shouting distance, he began looking for the bear den.

Although the bear den was one his father had known about, Simon knew they would have to search for it. It was hard to pinpoint exact locations in this ever-changing wilderness. Unless there was a clear-cut landmark such as a slough, a cut bank, a snag, or some other characteristic that did not change with the years, it was difficult to find a small hole that marked the entrance to a bear den.

Just then Simon heard a strange noise. It sounded metallic, like a drumming sound. Then he remembered, his father had taught him when they were in the woods to send signals by striking the ax head on a nearby tree. That was the sound he heard!

"Where are you?" he called out quietly.

"Over here," came the soft reply.

In a hurry to get to the spot Simon pushed his way through the brush. This was it! This was his first bear den!

When Simon got to the spot he was puzzled. All he saw was a hump on the side of the hill in the middle of some trees.

Out of breath, he gasped, "Where's the hole?"

"Down there," his father pointed.

Simon's heart thudded as he knelt down and peered into the small opening. Was there a bear in there? The narrow opening of the den descended into darkness, but there was no grass in the den entrance. He looked up at his father, "Is there one in there?"

Edwin moved closer, bent over, kneeled down near the entrance and listened. When he sat up his shoulders sagged.

"Nope, nothing in here. No door... no sound... no bear!"

Simon tried not to let his disappointment show.

Edwin stood and began making his way through the brush. Simon followed closely, trying hard to spot something that might be another bear den. Finally his father slowed, circled a small hill, then stopped and pointed to a small depression in the ground. Again they listened, then knelt down and looked for a grass door. Simon could see his father was disappointed.

"Nope, nothing here either. Too bad, too. Two years ago we got one in here."

"Yeah, but I wasn't with you then," Simon reminded him.

"You were too young," his father replied. "Finding bears is man's work. Not for women or kids. You're big enough now, but we can't find a good den. That's the way it is. When Mr. Bear is ready, he will let you know where he is."

Simon's heart sank. You had to be lucky to find a den with a bear in it. Simon knew luck was important, but there were other important things for a hunter. He had to know the old ways as well as the more modern ones. He had to work hard on the hunt and not give up easily. But he had done everything his father asked. He had packed the dogsled with all they needed. He had hooked up the dogs. He had been quiet in the woods as they searched for bear dens. What more could he do?

As they made their way back to where the dogs were chained Edwin said, "We get much more snow and we won't be able to find the bear dens this year because the snow will cover everything up. Let's make a fire and have some tea before we head back."

When the fire was ready Edwin propped the moose ribs up to cook and put the tea pot on to boil. Neither one spoke, but both father and son knew they shared their disappointment. They knew that's the way it was when you were looking for bears after freeze up. There was just a brief window of time when you could get out before the winter snows came and covered all sign of bears. Then winter began—the cold season. Denned bears would not be hunted anymore until next fall, a whole year away.

Hoping to change the somber mood, Simon asked, "Dad, could you tell a story? You know, one of those old ones about the animals?"

"How 'bout the one about beaver?" Edwin responded. He took a sip of tea and began.

Long time ago back when animals could talk like people, one cold windy day a porcupine sat by the riverbank crying. She was crying because she wanted to go to the other side of the river to eat birch and cottonwood, but she couldn't swim.

Pretty soon a mink came by and asked, "Setsugal, what are you crying for?"

Setsugal said she wanted to get to the other side of the river to eat. The mink said, "I will take you across Setsugal. Hop on."

Setsugal answered, "I can't ride on your tail. It's just like a stove poker and I might fall off and drown." So the mink went away.

Setsugal began crying again and pretty soon a muskrat came along. He asked, "What you crying for, Setsugal?" She explained again that she wanted to go across the river to eat birch and cottonwood. When he said, "Get on my tail, I will take you across," she replied, "Your tail is too small and round, just like a stove poker and I would fall off it and drown."

Finally along came a beaver and when she explained what she wanted to do he said, "Get on my tail and I'll take you across." So she got on the beaver's broad tail, but she picked up her hot iron cooking pot to take along. About halfway across the river, Setsugal could hold the pot up no longer so she set it down on the beaver's tail. The beaver, feeling the pain on his tail, gave it a good slap and flipped Setsugal off. The porcupine, she drowned. And that's how the beaver got his black tail.

"That's a good one, Dad! You think maybe I could set beaver traps this year?"

"I think you're about old enough for that," Edwin nodded. He looked at the darkening afternoon sky, finished the rest of his tea and said, "Well, I think we'd better head home. It looks like snow and besides, it's gonna get dark pretty soon."

Sitting in the sled behind the dog team as it bounced along the rough trail, Simon wondered, "Will I ever get a bear?" He had been to bear parties, eaten the freshly cooked bear meat, and listened to the stories the older men told. He had watched other men and boys accept the compliments with modesty as they celebrated with a potlatch for the bear. How he longed to be the one who supplied the meat for the bear party—proving he was a real Koyukon man. When would that be?

As they neared the village Simon smelled the wood smoke from the chimneys. Lights winked in the log cabin windows. It was snowing harder now and he brushed the snow from his parka. When they pulled into their dog yard he jumped out and helped his father unhook the dogs, chain them to their stakes, and feed them. The dogs had worked hard today and now they were glad to get their meal of cooked salmon.

Shaking the soft snow off their clothes, Simon and his father entered their warm cabin where his sisters eagerly asked, "You get anything?"

"Nope, not today. Mebbe next time." Edwin replied. "We saw some dens, but no luck this time. Maybe we'll just have to wait until next year."

"Too bad, but you know how it is with finding sis— the bear," Simon's mother responded. "You just have to be lucky. I bet you fellas would like some of this moose meat. You must be hungry." The warm room felt good. The smell of food made Simon's mouth water. He was ready to eat! He took off the extra layers of clothes he had worn and washed his hands in the washbasin nearby. Sitting down at the table he helped himself to a bowl of the steaming stew from the large pot on the table.

Simon hungrily downed the meat and vegetables. For dessert he spread a cold hotcake with butter and jam. What about his friends who had also gone out looking for bears today? Had they been lucky?

It had been a long day. With the warm room and the good food, Simon's head nodded forward.

"Simon, you can't sleep here. Go to bed," his mother said.

"Yeah, I am kinda tired, but I'd like to find out if any of those other fellas got a bear."

"You can find that out later."

Simon pulled off his shirt and pants and climbed into bed.

*   *   *

Monday morning at breakfast Simon heard his father say, "The radio says we're gonna get more snow for the next couple of days. Looks like bear season is over for this year."

Simon gulped his Tang and shoved bites of hotcakes into his mouth. He wondered, When will I get a bear? Not this year, I guess.

"Simon, hurry up. Your sisters are leaving for school. You don't wanna be late."

Simon grabbed his coat and hat from the pegs beside the door and followed his sisters outside. The cold air shocked him awake. Even though it was still dark he could see by the porch light several inches of new snow had fallen overnight, and more was coming down. He grinned. Bear season might be over, but dog mushing was just starting!

After walking the short distance to the school, Simon entered the warm building, shook the snow off his clothes, and hung up his jacket and hat. Then he kicked his feet together to knock the snow from his skin boots and slid into his seat in the classroom.

He turned to the boy seated behind him, "Ralph, you guys get anything yesterday?"

"No, nothing. I don't know about anybody else. Looks like the season is over for us."

"Maybe so—but we can start running dogs now."

Just before the close of the school day Simon's teacher, Mr. Kelly, shuffled through the stack of spelling papers the students had turned in. He looked up and said, "Simon you'll have to stay in until you finish your work." Simon finished in a hurry because he wanted to get outside and drive his dog team to get ready for the Christmas dog races. He had only a couple of months to get ready.

CHAPTER 2

THE RACE

The sun inched above the horizon about ten o'clock on Saturday morning, but Simon had been up long before that. This was the day of the kids' dogsled race! He had been practicing with his team each day of the week long Christmas vacation, and he knew every bump and bend in the five-mile course.

The cold air struck Simon as he stepped out of the cabin and the steam from his breath made clouds in the air that joined the smoke billowing up from the wood stoves of the village's log cabins. The temperature stood at zero, clear and cold, just right for dog racing. As he approached the dog yard the dogs, anxious to go for a run, set up a clamor, barking, jumping, howling, and straining at their chains. "I know, I know, you all want to go!"

Simon felt a dog's nose nudge his leg. "Okay, Queenie, you and Prince are gonna be my leaders today!" Simon hesitated only a moment before settling on a dog with big, pale blue eyes, "Now, Blue, you get to run in swing position behind them." Those were his favorites, the three he had practiced with, and the ones that knew him the best. "Pretty soon we're gonna run and this time it won't just be for practice!"

Simon finished setting out the harnesses and lines for hitching up the dogs. Their dogs were important since his father earned most of his money trapping, and his trap lines extended as much as twenty-five or thirty miles. To be able to tend the traps for mink, marten, wolf, wolverine, beaver, and otter, he had to check them at least twice a week. The money his dad got for the furs bought things they needed from the store. His gear ready, Simon hurried back to the cabin to eat and get warm clothes on for the race.

It was nearly noon and though the race wouldn't start for half an hour or so, Simon decided to hook up the dogs and get ready. As he drove his team down to the frozen river racecourse Simon passed people walking out to the riverbank to watch the races. They had built a huge bonfire and from their vantage point high on the bank, they would be able to stay warm while watching the teams go out and return to the finish line.

Once on the river, Simon joined several of his friends with their teams. They were bundled up against the cold and he could see the excitement in their eyes. He would be racing against both boys and girls aged ten to twelve. Each one would use a team of three dogs. Younger kids raced with one dog over a much shorter course. The adults used as many dogs as they felt they could control—sometimes as many as sixteen or eighteen. Contestants would draw for their starting positions before the race and they would start out two minutes apart. The person with the fastest time on the course would win. Judges had stopwatches to time each team from start to finish.

Soon it was Simon's turn to draw. Closing his eyes

tight, he reached into the coffee can and pulled out a slip of paper. He opened his eyes and looked at the number —five! Not the best position, but not the worst either. He would have to worry about passing and getting passed by other teams.

He pulled his team into the number five position, turned his sled upside down to act as a brake for the eager dogs, and sat on it. He would start just after Ralph, his best buddy, but the team he was most worried about was in the number six position—Gary's. Gary had a good team that was ready for the race. Simon had seen him practicing after school and during vacation.

Simon watched Ralph take off, then moved his own sled into the starting chute. The timer yelled, "Five... four... three... two... one, GO!" Simon was off, two minutes behind Ralph. The racecourse covered about five miles— up the river, across two sand bars, around an island, and then back to the main river to where they had started. Simon hoped his practice runs over the course would pay off. He knew the danger spots to look for—the bumps on the sand bars and the low branches from the trees on the island. But this time the race was for real! His heart pounded and his breath came in great gulps.

Standing on the sled runners Simon yelled to encourage the dogs to speed up, and he clapped his beaver skin mitts together, although he knew that they were pulling their best already. All dogs pull well at the first—they love running! It's toward the end of the race when they are tired that they slow down. As he listened to the hiss of the snow on the sled runners and felt the sting of the cold air on his face, he took a deep breath and let it out slowly. This was really fun!

Now on the second bar, Simon could see Ralph ahead. He was gaining on him! He urged the dogs on and began pumping with one foot to help speed the sled forward. Ralph was now just a short distance ahead. Simon was puzzled how he had caught up so soon. Suddenly he spotted a moose just off the trail, and Ralph's dogs were heading for it. As Ralph pushed on the brake with his foot and struggled to stop his dogs, Simon yelled at his own dogs who held firmly to the trail and sped by. His call, "Good luck!" was swallowed by the barking of Ralph's excited dogs. Simon wished he could help, but he knew Ralph had a better chance of getting control of his team without anyone helping. Besides, he didn't want to slow down. Now he just had to go around the island and back on the river. This was the best trail yet, evenly packed and smooth.

Confident as he rounded the island, Simon looked for another team to pass but he saw none. Then, glancing over his shoulder, he saw a team. It could be Ralph, but what if it's Gary? Simon urged his dogs on. "Come on, let's go!" Now the other team was on the river too, and it was gaining. It had to be Gary! Simon continued pumping with one foot, but it was no help. Gary kept gaining. Then Simon heard the call, "Trail!" He knew what to do. He had to pull off the trail, stop, and let them go by. He also knew this was the most dangerous part. What if the two teams got into a fight? He pushed down hard on the sled brake and stopped his team.

Gary's leaders moved by Simon's sled and began passing his dogs. Suddenly Queenie and Prince lunged at the passing team. Simon was nearly jerked off the sled as the dogs began to fight. In an instant both Gary and Simon were among their dogs, grabbing collars, pulling on lines and separating their teams. Finally they got them apart and Gary led his team back to the trail and took off. Simon straightened his lines, jumped on his sled runners and followed.

Simon's team now kept up with Gary's, but he knew he was behind in time. He looked up and could see the people on the bank cheering them on. He began running behind the sled, hanging on with his hands, and pushing for all he was worth. He crossed the finish line and suddenly it was over. He felt disappointed and tired as he drove his team up the bank and to the dog yard by his house. His sisters helped him unhook the dogs and chain them in their places.

"How did you do, Simon? What was your time?" Sonja asked excitedly, her dark eyes dancing.

"I dunno. Not too good," Simon responded. "Gary beat me."

"Yeah, we saw it," Rosie said as she hung her head and tugged on one of her braids.

When the dogs had each been rewarded with a piece of dry fish, Simon and his sisters hurried down the path to the community hall where Chief Henry would announce their times and places. Simon's shoulders sagged. He knew Gary had beaten him and he was sure that at least half of the other racers had too.

He slowed down and stopped. "I don't think I'll go down to the hall," Simon said.

"Oh, come on," Rosie urged. "You won't even know who won."

"Well, I know I didn't," he muttered.

"Come with us," Sonja begged, tugging at his sleeve.

Simon was curious to find out who won, even if it wasn't him. Besides, he wanted to see how Ralph got his dogs away from the moose. He followed his sisters down the trail and soon they joined the crowd in the hall.

"With a time of twenty-five minutes and seven seconds, first-place goes to Gary!" The crowd clapped as Gary walked up to get his prize money, ten dollars, and a blue ribbon. Simon looked at the floor, then joined in the clapping, hoping nobody would think he was a bad sport.

"Second-place, with a time of twenty-seven minutes and four seconds goes to Simon!" Simon could hardly believe his ears! He jumped to his feet. His legs felt rubbery as he walked out to the middle of the floor and shook hands with Chief Henry who handed him his five-dollar prize money and red ribbon. As he made his way back to his seat he pushed back the shock of dark hair that had fallen across his face and a huge grin spread from ear to ear.

"I guess I didn't do so bad after all," he thought happily.

Finding Ralph in the crowd, he asked, "How'd you get away from that moose?"

Grinning, Ralph replied, "After I got up to the team I just told them that I was gonna eat 'em for dinner if they didn't get back on the trail. I guess they believed me, 'cause they went back. 'Course it didn't hurt that the moose ran off too. I should have used a different leader.

That Blackie, he runs good, but he chases everything he smells." Simon joined Ralph's laughter.

"Next time I'm gonna practice harder," Ralph added.

"Yeah, me too," Simon said, draping his arm around Ralph's shoulders.

CHAPTER 3
THE POTLATCH AND DANCE

Simon pushed open the door to the house and stepped inside. His mother's voice greeted him, "How'd you do in the race?"

"Not too bad, I guess. I got second place. Gary beat me but I got this ribbon and five bucks. I gotta practice more so next time I can beat him." Seeing two huge pots of steaming moose meat on the Yukon stove, he asked, "What are those for, Mom?"

"You were so interested in the dog race you forgot all about the potlatch tonight," Mom said.

She was right. He had forgotten. Now he began to get hungry just thinking about it. The Christmas potlatch was one of the biggest feasts of the year. Others were held to greet visitors, for persons who had died, the end of school, and to celebrate other holidays like Thanksgiving and New Years. The potlatch was a custom many Indian groups in Alaska had been celebrating for generations.

Long ago people did not live in villages because there was not enough food to support large groups of people. In the winter they lived in camps along the frozen rivers where they fished and hunted for moose or caribou to feed their families. But in midwinter, when the frigid days were the shortest, the nights longest, and outside activities the least, potlatches were held. Families from up and down river would gather in a central location for several days to feast, visit, tell stories, sing, and dance.

When Simon and his family entered the log community hall around 5 o'clock, the aroma of food made his mouth water. The women in the village had prepared the food. Each woman seemed to have her specialty: Big Sophie's was moose head soup, Catherine's was cooked bear meat, Shirley's was moose ribs, and his mom's was moose stew. The women brought their contributions in large pots and placed them on clean tarps in the center of the split log floor.

Simon looked over the huge amount of food. Moose head soup and caribou meat steamed in large washtubs. Chunks of bear meat were piled high on a platter. There were thick slabs of still frozen bear fat as well. Roast lynx meat in thick slices filled a pan. The bear and lynx meat would be served only to men since it was considered "bad luck" for women to eat. Indian ice cream, made with pounded dry fish, fat, sugar, and blueberries was heaped in another large bowl. In addition, a lot of food had been bought from the store. Cases of canned fruit, Pilot Bread, cartons of cigarettes, boxes of cigars, sacks of candy, and cases of pop were stacked ready to be distributed. There were homemade cakes, pies and cookies. At the end were huge pots of hot coffee and tea, and jugs of Kool-aid for the kids.

Simon and Ralph found places with the other kids on the floor in front of their parents who sat on benches next to the wall. He reached back and tapped his mother's leg, "Did you bring dishes for me?" Smiling, his mother handed him a plate, bowl, and spoon.

Everyone became quiet. When he turned around Simon saw the oldest man in the village, Chief Henry, standing up to speak.

When Chief Henry finished speaking quietly in Koyukon, Simon's father stood to translate. "Chief Henry, he says he wants to thank you all for bringing all this good food to the potlatch. He also says that it is good for us all to get together in friendship and forget our quarrels with our neighbors. It has been a good year for us and we need to give thanks for good luck. He hopes that next year will be a good year too and that everything goes good for us."

Simon could understand a little of what Chief Henry said, but he wished he knew more of the Koyukon language. He was proud his father understood every word Chief Henry said and had the honor of translating for the younger people.

Next the Episcopal priest got up. Everyone stood while he blessed the food and the crowd. After everyone sat down the noise in the hall increased as the young men began to pass out the food. First they served the children, next the old people, and finally the younger adults. Everyone was served equal portions of food and until it was all gone.

As Bergman put a big chunk of bear meat on Simon's plate he smiled and said, "You gotta eat bear meat if you want to be lucky and find a bear!"

Simon grinned up at him and took a big bite of the meat. "Boy that is good!" He watched the pile of meat in front of him grow, and soon there were crackers, candy, cookies, cake and a bowl full of soup.

Simon and Ralph giggled as they tried to out-eat each other. Soon both were groaning with full stomachs. The cigars and cigarettes went to the adults. Last to be passed was the gum and candy for the kids. Sure that he couldn't eat another bite, Simon passed the rest of his food to his mom. She would put it in a box to take home to be eaten later.

Everyone gathered their containers full of leftover food and prepared to leave. Soon only the smell would linger in the hall to remind people of the potlatch. Simon took a deep breath. He loved potlatches! Food always tasted the best when you were surrounded by your family and friends!

As he walked out the door, someone called, "Don't forget! Dance in about two hours!

*   *   *

As Simon and his sister Rosie walked back to the hall in the dark they looked up at the star-laden sky. It was a crisp, cold night. Simon felt he could almost touch the silvery crescent moon that hung on the horizon. He looked up at the constellations—Orion, the Little Dipper, and the Big Dipper. Carefully following the two pointer stars in the lip of the Big Dipper, he found the North Star in the handle of the Little Dipper. It was nearly straight up from where he stood. As he looked to the northern horizon he saw the northern lights moving higher in the sky in long waves of white and greenish light.

"Dad told us that long ago they believed the spirits were angry when they sent the lights out at night," Simon told Rosie. Rosie hugged her arms to herself and shivered a little. It was cold now and the snow squeaked loudly as they walked. This was no time for hunting. The animals could hear you long before you got within range.

They reached the hall and Simon pushed the door open. As they entered the room a large cloud of white vapor spilled down on the floor and spread out as the cold air met the warmth of the building.

"Shut the door," someone called out. Simon grinned and pushed the door closed. He grabbed the broom propped by the door and dusted the snow off his boots. He felt a surge of pride as he looked down at the new boots his mother had made to start the New Year. The boots had moose-hide soles and calfskin uppers with wolverine and beaver fur trimming the tops. There was no doubt in his mind that his mother was one of the best boot makers in the village.

As he stood the broom against the wall Simon looked across the hall and saw the old men and women sitting together against the far wall. It was always this way. He saw his grandparents smiling at him and he nodded and smiled back. His grandparents had been born in small log houses that were half underground. He remembered his grandmother telling him they were lucky if they had a kerosene lamp traded to them by the white traders. If not, stone lamps fueled by animal fat provided light. They also knew what real hunger meant. She told him how, in hard times, some people had been forced to boil and eat the rawhide in their snowshoes. If they did not prepare for the long winter people might starve to death. That is why winter was called "the hungry time."

How different things were now! They lived in large log cabins that were well heated by wood stoves. Light came from electricity furnished by the village light plant. No one in this village knew what real hunger meant unless they got caught out on the land. Now with rifles, boats with outboard motors, dog teams, and snow machines, they could get meat or fish almost any time of the year. And they could also buy food from the store. Now the mail plane came twice a week hauling mail, freight, and passengers to the village. The health aide had daily contact with a doctor by radio to diagnose people's medical problems, and planes could be sent to take emergency cases to the hospital. They could listen to Anchorage and Fairbanks radio stations too, so they knew what was going on in Alaska and the rest of the world.

Because life was so much different now, Simon's grandmother had told him it was important for the people to keep some of the old ways. That was their link from the past to the future. The old time songs and dances were part of that link. And, Simon thought, so was bear hunting!

The singing began and Simon turned to see some of the women walking out onto the floor, unrolling a long bolt of cloth. They moved their hands and arms in time to the music while holding the cloth, with the old men and women singing. This was the scarf dance. At the end of each year this dance honored people who had died during the year. When someone died in the village there was a big potlatch. Then at the end of the year a special dance was held and belongings of the people who had died were given away.

When the dance ended the adults began spreading things out on the floor. Simon recognized them as belonging to Gary's grandfather, Ambrose, who had died recently. His traps, clothes, radio, dog harnesses, all his tools, and snowshoes were spread out. His closest relatives then passed these things out to his friends and to people they felt needed them. Everyone in the hall was given something. Simon was given a pair of new gloves. He felt sad for Ambrose's family as he remembered sitting in his grandparents house and listening to Ambrose telling stories. As Simon looked at the gloves he wondered how long this custom would continue. He would take care of the gloves.

After that ceremony two young men brought out their guitars and another got a violin and they began to play modern western style music. Younger people began to dance, but the old ones did not. They watched and seemed to enjoy themselves, but they did not dance to this new music. Simon watched for while, then he decided to go home. He was tired.

CHAPTER 4

BEAVER TRAPPING

After the Christmas and New Year's festivities, the short days passed rapidly. Simon watched the sun rise from just barely above the horizon in late December to a much higher place in the sky now. As the days got longer, village men turned their attention to beaver trapping. Now that he was twelve, Simon could legally trap beaver, and his father said they would trap together. Simon wished he didn't have to go to school because that meant they would only be able to go out to check his beaver sets on the weekends. When his father changed the calendar to February, Simon knew it was time. Finally the weekend arrived and early Saturday morning they drove their eight-dog team out of the village to his father's trapline.

"Where will I make my sets, Dad?" Simon asked eagerly.

"You'll take the beaver houses closest to town on my line so that when it gets lighter after school you can go down and check them if you want," Edwin said. Simon nodded. He had been on his father's beaver trapline many times before, but only to watch. This time he would make his own sets.

The dogs pulled hard. Even though the trail itself was packed, about four inches of fresh light snow lay on top of it. If the team got off the trail the dogs could sink clear up to their necks in the soft snow. Then his father would have to put on snowshoes and walk in front of them to pack the snow down to lead them back on the trail. But the lead dogs were smart, they knew where the trail was and they stayed on it.

About eight miles out of the village they came to a large open area and Edwin braked the team to a stop. "What are we stopping for?" Simon asked.

"To make your first set. See the house over there?" His father pointed. Simon looked, but try as he might he could not see anything that might be a beaver house.

"Right there," his father pointed to a small mound about fifty yards away.

"How do you know that's a beaver house?" asked Simon.

"When you live around here as long as I have you remember the important things, especially if it's something that means money!" Edwin chuckled.

Simon looked carefully, but he could only see a few branches sticking out of the top of the mound. To him it looked like brush from anyplace, not necessarily from a beaver house. His dad was really smart!

Simon untied the shovel and ice chisel from the sled, put on his hand-made snowshoes, and made his way to where his father was already searching for the feed pile. During the fall, the beaver cut birch and cottonwood branches to store as food for the winter and pulled them near the beaver house in the water. Later they would not be able to break through the thick ice to get food. "Dad, how do beaver live all winter?"

Edwin smiled and began, "The beaver is a hard-working man. He works all summer building dams and improving his house. By fall-time he has to gather enough food to last him and his family all winter, so by freeze-up he's ready for a rest. By now Mr. Beaver is fat and his skin is good. This is his resting time of year, when he takes it easy. We can learn a lot of lessons from the beaver, like get ready for winter and you won't have to worry about getting hungry."

"But how do they stay warm?"

"Well, the inside of their house is above the water line and their houses are thick. If you try to dig into that house you'd see it would be over three feet thick and packed tight with mud and sticks. Inside they have a small room full of shavings they use for a dry bed. Besides they have thick fur. That's what we're after."

"When they come out to eat, how long can they stay under the ice?"

"I dunno, but long enough for them to cut a stick from the feed pile and get back. Since the feed pile is close to the house they can go out, chew off a branch, and take it back into the house to eat." To Simon the tips of the feed pile protruding through the ice and snow looked like any other brush pile, but to the beaver it represented food and life.

"Do they eat all of this brush?" Simon asked.

"The small twigs they eat whole, but on the larger branches they will just eat the bark and leave the rest, but it also depends on how many live in there. How many do you think?"

Simon shrugged his shoulders, so his father continued, "Usually one family, the parents and maybe two or three kids. When the babies are born in the spring the others leave to make their own families."

Locating the feed pile, they moved to one side of it close to the house. "We'll make our set here," his father said.

After they shoveled three feet of snow off the ice, Edwin handed Simon the ice chisel. "Here, you test the ice, Simon. Listen for a hollow sound."

Simon lifted the tall metal ice chisel and struck the ice. Chunk! He struck again with the instrument. In the old days, Simon knew, an ice chisel was made of horn or bone and attached to a strong piece of wood.

Simon continued to shovel the snow away and strike the ice in different places until finally he heard a hollow chunking sound.

"There. That's the place to make your hole."

"How come?" Simon asked.

"That's where the beaver goes back and forth to and from his house. The hollow sound is made by the air the beaver breathed out that's trapped under the ice."

Simon began chopping with the chisel. Even though the chisel was sharp it was still hard work. He had to cut a hole about eighteen inches in diameter and, although the chips flew, it took him about twenty minutes to cut through the ice and shovel the chips away.

"Boy! This is hard work," Simon said as he finished shoveling all the ice chips out of the water.

"You had an easy time," his father answered. "The ice was only a foot thick. Sometimes it might get two feet thick—or even more!"

While Simon had been cutting the hole in the ice his father had snowshoed over to the edge of the pond where he cut small green cottonwood trees about two inches thick for the bait. While his father cut them into pieces about two feet long, Simon attached the toggle, or end of the snare he was going to use, to a thick dry spruce branch his father provided. He then made a loop with the snare, making sure that it was nearly round and about ten inches in diameter. Holding the dry branch up he tested to see how the snare hung.

Following his father's instructions, Simon carefully lowered the snare into the water so that the metal slide was located just a few inches below the ice. Then he set another snare on the other side of the hole. Once the snares were in place he shoveled snow into the hole and stuck the two cottonwood sticks of bait straight down between the snares. Simon hoped the beaver, coming to his feed pile, would notice two freshly cut sticks and, because they looked good to eat, he would swim over for a taste and get caught.

His set made, Simon shoveled more snow into the set hole. He knew that putting the snow in the hole would prevent the bait from slipping down too far and also keep the ice from becoming too thick. Snow was a good insulator and the ice would not get more than a few inches thick with snow in it.

As they loaded their tools on the sled, Simon asked, "How long do you think that took?"

"I dunno, maybe an hour. At this rate we'll have to hurry before it gets dark. But don't worry, you'll get faster with practice."

In all they made eight sets similar to the first one. As they headed home in the bluish twilight, Simon relaxed wearily in the sled. "Boy! I sure didn't think that it would be that much work."

"In the old days you would have worked twice as hard for half that number of sets 'cause we didn't have modern equipment. You did pretty good, though, for your first time."

Simon felt contented. Although his dad had only said a few words, he could hear the pride in his voice.

"When will we check our sets?"

"Next Saturday will be okay, I guess. That'll give Mr. Beaver plenty of time to get caught!"

CHAPTER 5

THE CATCH

The week seemed to take forever to pass. It was hard for Simon to keep his thoughts on schoolwork, and he daydreamed about the fat beavers his snares would catch. He woke early on Saturday morning and jumped out of bed. He used his thumb to rub a spot on the window clear of frost and looked out at the blue-tinged sky. Heavy clouds of smoke from the cabins hung over the village. It had to be colder than usual outside. When the temperature drops and there is no wind, the heavy cold air forces the smoke right down to the ground. Simon looked at the thermometer outside the window. Forty below zero. He went over to where his father was sleeping, and shook his shoulder "It's forty below. We gonna check my beaver sets today?"

Edwin squinted his eyes open, "How cold?"

"Forty below."

"That's pretty cold."

"Yeah, but we need to check my beaver sets today. If I caught one it could freeze in the ice, or an otter might get it." While freezing in might hurt the guard hairs of the pelt, the otter was the biggest worry.

Edwin stretched and sat up. "Well, let's get up and see what the temperature does in the next couple hours. Put some more wood in the stove. It's cold in here!"

After eating breakfast Simon kept his eye on the thermometer. As the sun's rays inched over the trees on the horizon, the temperature did warm up.

"Dad, it's only thirty-five below now. It's warming up. Can we go?"

Edwin smiled. Simon would pester him until he agreed to go. "Let's go and check just your snares. It shouldn't take too long—maybe a couple of hours because your sets are already made. It'll probably warm up some more and besides, we can't make any money staying here in the house. You'll have to dress up warm!"

Elated, Simon began pulling on layers of clothes. He pulled two pairs of pants over his long underwear, two shirts, his heavy sweater, a light nylon jacket, and his mother's beaver parka with a wolverine ruff on the hood. On his feet he put two pairs of wool socks, a felt boot liner and a pair of caribou skin boots that reached to his knees. He knew his feet would be warm because the caribou has hollow hair that insulates by keeping the heat in and the cold out. For his hands he chose a pair of heavy wool hand-knit gloves and his mother's big beaver mitts. This way he could take off the mitts and still keep his hands warm while checking the snares.

While Simon was struggling into his clothes his father was outside hooking up the dogs. When he finished he came back into the house, rubbing his hands together. "Adzoo!" the Koyukon word for "It's cold!" "Be sure to wear plenty of clothes. You don't wanna get cold sitting in the sled."

"Uh-huh," Simon replied.

By the time he got his beaver parka on along with all his other clothes, Simon looked like a fur man. He felt twice as big as he normally did. "Boy! It's sure hot in here," he said.

"Go outside and cool off," his mother said with a smile.

Outside Simon could make heavy clouds of vapor just by breathing hard in the cold air. The snow squeaked when he walked on it and the trees were covered with a thick frost rime.   Edwin had also put on his beaver parka, mitts, and caribou boots, and finished tying everything down in the sled. He turned to Simon, "Do you have everything?"

"I guess so."

"Okay, then jump on." He pulled the hook from its stake and they were off.

"Are you going to hold the dogs back?" Simon asked.

"Not now. We'll see how fast they go first. They know it's not a race."

The dogs seemed to sense that this cold weather could be dangerous and they moved quickly, but did not run. Sounds they made seemed twice as loud as normal. This was because the trail was frozen hard and the sound was reflected more easily. It was also very still. No wind or other noises muffled the sound they made, and even the hiss of the steel runners on the snow sounded loud to Simon.

When they arrived at the first beaver house, Simon jumped off the sled and danced around clapping his hands together to warm up. "Adzoo!" he exclaimed. He could hardly wait to thrust the ice chisel through the newly formed ice where his snares were. He helped his dad put the anchor for the sled around a small birch tree. Simon looked at the dogs as he walked past them. The fronts of their furry bodies were covered with frost that had formed as their breath condensed and froze. Frost also clung to Simon's fur parka hood. But he wasn't thinking about the cold now. His mind was on the set.

"You want me to cut the hole open?" His dad asked.

"I can do it," Simon said.

"Well, be careful then."

Simon didn't have to be told that if there was a beaver in the snare it would be just under the ice. If he rammed the sharp ice chisel through the ice into it, it would make a hole in the pelt. Each hole would reduce the value of a pelt by five dollars. He didn't want to ruin the pelt of the first beaver he might catch all on his own. Very carefully, he began chipping the ice from around the edges of the hole. Even though the ice was thinner now, it was still hard work. Finally he punched through the ice. Using the chisel as a feeler, he probed around gingerly.

"Dad, I can feel something rubbery under there. Could it be ...?"

"Maybe, but finish cutting the hole out carefully now, and then we'll see for sure," his father interrupted.

Simon freed the snare sticks and removed the ice chips with the shovel. Now came the test. He pulled up on the snare stick and up came the snare.... It was empty. "Gee, I thought it was my best set too," he said dejectedly.

"Try the other one."

As he grasped the other stick and began pulling Simon noticed a difference immediately. It was heavy. He pulled harder and out came the head, and then the body of a large beaver.

Simon's heart pounded. "That's a big one, yeah, Dad?"

"Uh huh. You got a nice one for your first try."

Quickly his father picked up the beaver and began rolling it in the snow. This would get rid of the water in its coat and keep it from freezing, so it would be ready to skin sooner.

Simon looked at his beaver. Its body was about two feet long. The tail added another foot to the length and was about five inches wide. Large webbed hind feet were as large as his father's hands and provided the main power for swimming. The front legs or "arms" as villagers called them, were much smaller, with fingers for putting sticks and other things into its mouth. It had four main front teeth, longer bottom ones, and shorter curved upper ones for cutting. Teeth for chewing were in the back. The fur, probably an inch thick, consisted of two parts, the dark under fur and the much lighter, longer guard hairs. Simon could see why there was a demand for this beautiful fur. He tried to lift the beaver. It was way heavier than he thought.

"You going to finish your set?" Simon was pulled from his thoughts by his father's voice.

"Should we keep the set here?"

"Yeah, I think so. We'll try to catch one more big beaver. Then we'll pull the set. We don't want to catch any of the small ones," his father answered. Beaver trappers tried to catch only adult beaver. That way there would be animals left for the future. Maybe someday Simon would inherit his father's trap line. He wanted animals to still be there then.

Simon attached the new snare to the dry stick and lowered it carefully into the hole, then did the same with the other one. After putting the fresh bait sticks in, he kicked snow into the hole, placed the bait down, and shoveled more snow on top. "Well, that takes care of that one," he declared, "only seven more to go!"

As they moved slowly around the trap line they were rewarded for coming out on this cold day. They caught four adult beaver. In the other sets, the wary animals had either taken the bait or had not come around.

By the time they arrived home it was dark and Simon was tired, but happy. He took off his winter clothes and helped himself to a big bowl of the moose stew that was bubbling on the stove. Then he curled up on the bed to rest a bit.

"Simon, wake up! We gotta skin the beaver." His father's voice jarred him awake.

Edwin looked at the beaver thawing on the floor. "If you're old enough to trap, you're old enough to skin," he grinned as he lifted the beaver up onto the kitchen table that he had covered with cardboard.

Simon picked up the knife, but hesitated. He had seen his father skin many beaver, but he'd never done it himself.

"Could you help me?"

"Okay, first you watch."

Simon watched carefully as his father began skinning, then grabbed a chisel-shaped bone tool, and used it to separate the skin from the fat. The skin came free remarkably fast and in about twenty minutes he was finished.

"Now you try the next one," his father told him.

With the sharp knife, Simon carefully slit the skin and began working the pelt loose. The beaver fat on his hands made them slippery so he wiped them on his pants and continued.

Next, Simon worked on the back, then finally the head, and he was done! Not one hole either! He glanced at the clock. It had taken him an hour, but he would get faster. In the meantime his father had skinned another one and was halfway through with the last.

"When I finish here, take these skins and three of the animals out to the cache. We'll stretch the skins later. We'll leave one animal in here overnight. Then tomorrow your mother will cut it up and we'll have beaver stew. You like that."

"When will Mom cook the tail?"

"Pretty soon, why?"

"Man, that's the best part!"

Later on Simon and his father stretched the skins on large four by four foot wooden stretchers. The beaver skin was nailed to these boards and carefully pulled outward toward the edge. When a skin was stretched and dried it looked like a large round circle of fur. His mother would use the smaller beaver skins and ones that had repaired holes in them to make parkas, hats, boot trim, or mitts for their family.

*   *   *

By the end of the season Simon had his limit, twelve good skins to sell. As he rolled them up in a bundle and put them in a gunnysack, ready to send to the fur buyer, he asked his father, "How much you think we'll get for these skins?"

"I don't know for sure. It depends on the market, but a super blanket should bring thirty-five dollars with less for the others because they're smaller."

Simon calculated his catch—a hundred and five dollars for three super blankets—and the rest should bring at least two hundred. "I might get three hundred dollars!"

The pelts hadn't been gone more than a few days when Simon began stopping by the post office after every mail plane. "Anything for me?" he'd ask the postmistress.

It was two long weeks before his check came. Clutching it in his hand he ran all the way home and burst into the house shouting, "Mom! Dad! I got three hundred seventy dollars for my beavers!"

After the whole family had examined the check, Simon handed it to his mother and said, "Here you keep this for me. I must be the richest boy in town now!"

His mother just smiled. She didn't want to discourage him now that he was so happy, but she knew it wasn't right for him to brag.

That night Simon lay on his bed thinking about what he could buy with the money. A new kicker or outboard motor, a shotgun, a rifle, a twenty-two, toys, comics.... He could think of so many things. He remembered that his father also had trapped beaver and, he too, had gotten money. In fact, Edwin had gotten six hundred fifty dollars, but Simon knew that money had to support the family until next fall unless his father got a job fighting forest fires or working for someone.

"Dad, you suppose it would be okay if I bought a twenty-two with my beaver money?"

"Sure, if you want, you could buy lots of twenty-twos with that money."

"No, I only want one." He paused, and added, "I'd like to take out the money for the twenty-two and give you and Mom the rest."

His father smiled, "It's your money."

"Well, I've been thinking. What does a kid like me need three hundred and seventy dollars for? I'd just spend it anyway."

"Okay, we'll look in the catalog for a good twenty-two for you in the morning." Edwin smiled to himself. He was proud of his son. Simon was beginning to think of others.

CHAPTER 6

GOING AFTER CARIBOU

The days in March grew longer and the sun warmed the air. The top layer of snow hardened so travel became easier and faster. Simon overheard his father tell his mother that he was planning to hunt caribou along with several other men from the village. "It'd be nice to have some fresh meat for a change," he heard his mother say. Simon longed to go along, but he knew he would not be able to go because he had to go to school. The weekend was just not long enough to go to the nearby mountains forty miles away to hunt and get back.

"When will you go out?" Simon asked his father.

"Next Friday, I think."

Simon's thoughts whirled. If he could talk Mr. Kelly into letting him miss a day of school, maybe he could go along! He ran to the teacher's house by the school and knocked on the door.

"Can I visit?"

"Sure, Simon, come in."

Simon went inside, sat down and pretended to be interested in what his teacher was talking about, but he was not fooling anyone.

"What's going on, Simon?" Mr. Kelly finally inquired.

"Well, I was just wondering how I was doing in school?"

"I think you're doing fairly well, why?"

"Dad just said he was going caribou hunting next Friday and well...I thought maybe I could go along if it was all right with you."

"Did your dad send you to ask me?" Mr. Kelly asked.

Simon hesitated. "No," he answered truthfully. He pushed back the lock of dark hair that had fallen across his eyes and looked up at Mr. Kelly.

Mr. Kelly paused long enough to make Simon begin to lose hope. "Well, if you went, would you make up the work you missed?"

"Yeah."

"And write a two-page paper telling about your hunt?"

Without hesitation, Simon answered, "Yeah!"

"Well then, Mr. Kelly laughed, "I guess it would be okay. You've never been caribou hunting before, have you?" Simon shook his head. "I'd sure like to go out there myself, but I can't. I have to be here in school. One more thing, don't tell the other kids about this or we might end up with no one in school!"

A broad grin spread across Simon's face. He was going caribou hunting! As he hurried home he thought about how he was going to ask his father. When he entered the house Edwin was at the table drinking coffee, hunting plans forgotten. Simon's words tumbled out, "Dad, Mr. Kelly said I can go caribou hunting with you!"

"What?"

"Mr. Kelly says I can go caribou hunting with you. Well, I mean, he said I could have Friday off to go with you if I make up the work I miss."

Simon's father hesitated, and then said, "You know what that means. We'd have to come back on Sunday."

"Yeah, but we'd have one day to hunt. And I've never been caribou hunting with you before."

"Okay I guess you can go." Edwin paused, "But you'll have to split wood for the time we're gone so that your mom has enough to keep the house warm."

Friday morning finally came and Simon was up ahead of everyone else. He looked at the clock. It was 6 a.m. and it was light already. If they hurried they could be gone before school started. He had already gotten his clothes, sleeping bag, and equipment ready the night before, but he just couldn't sleep anymore.

After building the fire he went outside to get the sled ready and to make sure the dogs had enough food for the three-day journey. Each dog would eat one dried salmon each day and get its water from the snow along the trail. He carefully laid the tarp over the top of the sled and began packing things into it. When he got back into the house his mother was making hotcakes. Simon piled several onto his plate and poured syrup on them. It might be many hours before he ate again.

After breakfast Simon and his father went out and finished loading their large sled. Then they began to hook up the dogs.

"How many will we take this time?" Simon asked.

"Fifteen, I think. We can't waste time on the trail and we want to be able to bring back caribou, if we get any."

They tied everything down on the sled and finished hooking up the dogs. Then Simon jumped on and made himself a place to sit on his moose-hide cushion. Edwin pulled the hook loose and shouted, "Hie!" to the eager dogs. They burst out of the yard and charged through town, but once on the river they began to pace themselves, as if they knew they were going for a long journey.

The sun broke the eastern horizon and warmed the air to ten degrees above zero. Spring weather meant the dogs had good footing for a faster journey, and the forty-mile trip up to the cabin was made with only one stop for tea. Simon was thankful for the stop, as three hours of sitting in the sled made him stiff as well as cold. While his father was gathering wood for the fire along the riverbank, Simon ran up and down the trail to warm up. Finally after a cup of hot tea and some of his mom's cookies he was warm and ready to go again.

Soon after their break they left the river and the trail wound up a small valley. Simon noticed a change in the country. Now, except in the sheltered valleys, there were no trees, just low bushes. Left behind were the black spruce trees, the birch and the willow, and the land of many lakes. They were now above the timberline. This was the closest he had ever been to the mountains that seemed so far away from the village.

"Dad, how come the caribou don't come closer to town so it would be easier to hunt them?"

"I dunno. Maybe they like the feed up here better. Long ago caribou used to come near to town sometimes, but now they don't."

Edwin pointed upward towards a little patch of stunted trees at the end of the valley ahead. "That's where we'll stay tonight. There's a trapping cabin up there with a stove in it. Nobody uses it much now except caribou hunters."

They reached the cabin in the late afternoon, the first to arrive. They unhooked the dogs, chained them to posts nearby, and carried their gear inside the cabin. Soon the others would come along with their dogs or snow machines. It was always this way. When one man decided to go on a long trip he would ask his friends or relatives to go too. It was safer because if someone got lost or had trouble, help was close. Simon and his father chose places to sleep on the floor next to the back wall, unrolled their sleeping bags, put their gear on top, and started a fire in the stove with wood that had been left in the cabin.

When they walked outside to feed the dogs, Simon looked up at the mountain.

"What do you see?" his father asked.

"I was wondering where the caribou are and how we'll get up that steep mountain."

"They're up on top and we'll get to them by going up that creek bed over there."

As he looked where his father was pointing he could see a small wrinkle in the mountain's white surface.

While he was feeding the dogs Simon heard snow machines approaching. The others had begun to arrive and he could see that all four had snow machines. Tony pulled up, turned his machine off, and pushed back the hood of his parka.

"When did you fellas leave?" Tony asked Simon.

"About eight, I guess."

"How long did it take you to get here?"

Simon thought a moment, then responded, "Dad said it took us nearly eight hours."

"You know how long it took us?"

Simon's father joined the conversation and asked, "How long?"

"Just about four hours and we weren't going fast either. Boy! These sno-gos are really good. You ought to get one," Tony declared.

"I dunno. We'll wait and see how many of you are ready to go back when I am on Sunday. Dogs don't break down like sno-gos. I know I can always get home with my dogs," Edwin said with a grin.

Laughing, they all went into the small cabin, and began to cook dinner.

"Are you going to tell us some of your stories tonight, Richard?" someone asked.

"I will if Steven and Jimmy will too. They both nodded their heads in agreement. Simon hoped dinner would be over soon since he loved to listen to the old-time stories.

After dinner, the men sat on the floor of the small log cabin and leaned back against the walls, sipping coffee. The gas lamp flickered, casting shadows across the room as the tales began. After Richard had finished his story one of the men turned to Jimmy, and said, "Jimmy, now its your turn."

Simon tried to stay awake for the story but the warm cabin, a full belly, and the day's exercise made him so sleepy he couldn't keep his eyes open. He crawled into his sleeping bag and immediately fell asleep.

CHAPTER 7
THE CARIBOU HUNT

"Simon...Simon, you gonna sleep all day?"

Simon opened his eyes and looked around the cabin. Everybody was up but him. Today they were going after caribou! The men were busy putting on their clothes and getting the fire ready to cook breakfast. Simon crawled out of his sleeping bag and joined them.

While they were eating their hotcakes, bacon and eggs, and drinking coffee, Jimmy said to Simon, "Why don't you come with me on my sno-go and sled, and your dad can go with Steven on his? That way you don't have to hook up dogs or worry about them when we get close to the caribou. You know how dogs get excited when they get around animals, especially now because there's lots of caribou up there."

Simon's father looked over at Jimmy, "You think you have room for us?"

"Sure, and we could make better time, too. Remember it's all uphill from here on."

"Yep, that's a good idea. We'll go with you fellas."

When they finished eating, the men put on their parkas and went out to gas up the snow machines and make sure everything was ready. Bright sunlight met Simon as he stepped out the cabin door and went over to his dogs. He knew they were eager to go. "You can't go this time, but we'll be back soon and maybe we'll bring back something for you to eat," he told them

"Simon, come on, let's go!"

"Okay," he shouted as he ran over to the sled behind the snow machine and jumped on the sled runners, hanging onto the sled's handlebar. They were off! Looking over his shoulder, Simon could see his father on another sled and the three snow machines coming behind them.

The little caravan of hunters climbed steadily up in the frozen creek bed. The only trees were a few stunted alders. Rocks jutted up everywhere and the snow machine drivers swerved back and forth to avoid hitting them and breaking the metal skiis.

The higher they climbed the more tracks Simon noticed. In some places the caribou had used their broad hooves to paw back the snow to get at their favorite winter food—lichens, or caribou moss.

Simon's mind wandered. His dad had told him these caribou were from the northern Arctic slope of the Brooks Range and had traveled a long way to get to this place to spend the winter. Why did they come here? Maybe the cold and wind farther north was the reason the caribou migrated. No one really knew why the salmon returned from their long journey to the place where they were born. People did not know exactly why the ducks and geese left and returned to the places they were born either, or how it all got started. Maybe it didn't really matter anyway. As long as they came back and provided food for the people in his village, that was what really counted.

He looked up and noticed Jimmy's arm pointing up the valley and saw…tiny brown specks in the distance. Caribou! When they got closer he could see there were about twenty in this nearby band. Their brown hair made them stand out against the white snow. Jimmy stopped his snow machine and while they were waiting for the others to catch up, Simon saw the caribou had stopped eating and were watching the snow machines approach. They seemed unafraid, and why should they be? With a two or three hundred-yard head start they could easily outrun any of their enemies, even wolves. So why should they fear these funny sounding, slow-moving machines?

When the snow machines were all together Jimmy said, "We'll try to surround them on that hill. That way we can get all we need. Shoot only what you can take back yourself. We won't have any trouble getting enough. Steven, you go around to the other side opposite me, and you boys go up on either side. I'll stay here and wait 'til you're ready and then we'll move in slowly. Be careful where you shoot!

The men drove the snow machines up the steep banks and soon disappeared from view. The only way Simon knew they were moving was from the muffled sound of the motors. Jimmy shut his engine off and turned to Simon. "You ever shoot a caribou?"

"No, I've never even seen a live one before this."

"You ever shoot a thirty-thirty?"

Simon hesitated. He had shot his dad's rifle last summer at a target. He remembered feeling the bruises from its kick for several days afterwards and he didn't want to shoot that kind of gun again anytime soon.

"Yeah, I shot my dad's thirty-aught-six," he answered slowly.

Jimmy unshouldered the battered thirty-thirty he was carrying on his back and handed it to Simon. "Go ahead, put a shell in the chamber."

Simon worked the lever action that took a shell from the magazine, placed it in the rifle's chamber, and put the safety on. The gun was ready.

Jimmy nodded, satisfied that Simon knew how to work the gun. "Since you've never shot a caribou and I've got to drive the snow-go, I want you to do the shooting. I'll stop when it's time to shoot. You jump off, rest the rifle on the uprights of the sled, and take your shot. Remember, try to shoot a little ahead of a running caribou. Try to hit them just behind the shoulder. If you can pick out the leader of the herd, shoot him first. The other animals won't know what to do then."

Looking up, they could see some of the other snow machines in position now. Jimmy started his snow machine, gave the signal and they began slowly moving toward the animals, closing the circle. The caribou were now getting nervous and began to run. Then they turned and began running toward Jimmy and Simon. Jimmy moved forward a bit and turned them, then stopped his snow machine. The animals, now thoroughly confused, were bunched up not fifty yards away, nervously looking around.

Jimmy shouted, "Shoot! Shoot! Shoot before they run!"

Simon threw the gun to his shoulder, rested on the sled, pulled back on the hammer and sighted in on the largest animal of the bunch. Bang! Miss! Quickly he levered another shell into the chamber and pulled the gun slightly in front of the moving animal he had missed, and squeezed. At his second shot the animal stumbled, then fell to his knees.

"I got him. I got him!" In his excitement Simon forgot all about shooting more caribou.

Jimmy grabbed the gun from him, kneeled down and shot twice more at the now running caribou. Each time he fired a caribou fell.

"Good shots," Simon said in admiration. "I don't know if I'll ever be able to shoot like that."

"You will. All it takes is practice," Jimmy grinned.

"Well, I guess that's all we can haul back," he said as he re-loaded his rifle and placed it on the sled.

The other hunters had closed in and now were shooting. When they had each shot one or two, they allowed the caribou to break through the circle and escape. Simon watched them disappear over the hill.

"Gee, I didn't think it'd be that easy," Simon said, almost disappointed that it was all over so quickly.

"In the old days it wasn't," Jimmy answered. "With just bows and arrows and spears, they'd try to drive them past certain spots where they could get a close shot.

Sometimes we would put on a caribou skin and head and try to sneak up on the herd, but that way we might only get one or two before they ran away. Now with snow-gos for help we can get as many as we want, but we never kill more than we need."

The men drove their snow machines close to the animals and began to butcher them.

"Man, I didn't know these caribou were so small," Simon said.

"Well, they're a lot smaller than moose, that's for sure. But they sure taste good and it's good to have fresh meat at this time of year," Jimmy replied.

When they finished cutting up the animals Simon and Jimmy loaded two of them on the sled, tied them down, and headed back to camp. Jimmy would return later to pick up the other animal, as this was all their sled would carry.

Before they went back, they drove clear to the top of the mountain to look around. From there they saw several herds of caribou. Simon saw many rocks and even bare frozen ground that the wind had stripped clear of its snow cover. Looking south towards the village, he could see the frozen river where he lived. There were thousands of small white puddles he knew were really frozen lakes. He looked for his village, but it was too far away to see.

The wind came up and the snow began to swirl around them. "Aren't you glad you don't live up here?" asked Jimmy.

"Yeah, that wind sure is cold, but we'd have lots to eat!" Simon's dark eyes sparkled as he replied.

Jimmy laughed and said, "Not all year around. These caribou just spend the winter here, and then they migrate back north. We'd better head back for camp and see how that fresh caribou tastes."

Simon had forgotten all about food. At the thought of fresh meat he realized his stomach was empty. "Yeah, I'm hungry now!"

Jimmy dug into his pack in the sled and handed Simon a large cracker. "Here take this. That should hold you 'til we get down to camp."

Eagerly Simon bit into the round Pilot Bread cracker. He was so hungry he didn't miss the peanut butter or jam he usually spread on them at home.

That evening the men cooked a huge meal of fresh fried caribou, onions and potatoes. Everyone ate until he could eat no more. Then the men relaxed and began to tell stories again, but Simon could barely keep his eyes open for the first story.

The next morning Simon and his dad loaded their gear and the meat from the two caribou they had gotten onto their sled and prepared to return home. "Yep, Edwin," Jimmy said," I think your boy is going to make a fine hunter. He'll probably be ready to look for a bear next fall."

"Well, I dunno. He still has a lot to learn," Edwin responded, then looked over at Simon and smiled. "But he does seem lucky, and he sure wants to catch a bear too!"

Simon just grinned. He knew those words were high compliments and he had many things to think about on the trip home.

As Simon and his father left camp Jimmy called out, "After we get the rest of the meat, we'll follow you home, but I bet we beat you there!"

"Those sno-gos are pretty good," Simon said, "Maybe we should get one, Dad."

"Yeah, they're good all right. But they cost a lot and you gotta buy gas, oil, and spare parts for them." Edwin paused, "And sno-gos break down, not like dogs."

"But dogs slow down when they're tired," Simon added hopefully.

"We'll see," his father replied.

CHAPTER 8

THE ACCIDENT

Spring was coming. March and April flew by. Since it didn't get dark until after ten o'clock at night, Simon had time to play outside after school. It seemed like everyone in the village was working—mending fishnets, repairing or building canoes, and working on boats and outboard motors. They were getting ready for "breakup," when the ice in the river thaws enough to break into thousands of pieces and goes churning down toward the Bering Sea, leaving the river as a highway to fishing, hunting, and to other places.

The days grew longer and the sun's warmth melted the snow that covered the land. There were pools and streams of water everywhere in the village. Simon and his friends made dams and ditches in the sandy soil, and floated small sticks and homemade boats down the streams. Often Simon attached a small boat to a string, tied the string to a stick he held, and pulled the boat through the larger puddles. He had a pair of knee-high rubber boots, but he did not always wear them, and so he often had wet feet.

Late one spring evening after Simon had fallen and gotten wet playing in the water, he went to bed early, then woke up in the middle of the night. "I'm cold," he mumbled. "I need more blankets." He didn't see any close by so he curled up and went back to sleep.

When he woke up in the morning Simon felt awful. His head hurt and he ached all over. "Simon, get up and get ready for school!"

"I don't feel so good, Mom."

"What's the matter?"

"I don't know. I just hurt all over."

"Well, get up and we'll see how you feel after breakfast."

"But I don't want any breakfast. All I want is more covers for my bed. It's cold in here."

Seeing that he was not pretending, Simon's mother put another blanket on his bed, and went on fixing the family's breakfast. When his sisters were ready to leave for school, she said, "Okay, you kids go to school and tell the teacher Simon is sick today."

She turned to Simon and felt his forehead. "You feel warm. Let's give you an aspirin. That'll make you feel better."

Simon swallowed the aspirin and went to sleep. When he woke again he was surprised at how quiet it was in the house. No kids, just Mom and Dad. The radio wasn't even on. His mother was sewing moose-hide slippers and his dad was looking through the Sears catalog.

Simon decided it was no fun to be sick, so when his two sisters came home for lunch he got out of bed, pulled his clothes on and said, "I think I feel good enough to go to school now." He knew his mom and dad probably wouldn't let him play out after school if he hadn't felt well enough to go to school that day. Simon ate a little soup for lunch, then announced to his parents, "I'm gonna go to school." He still didn't feel well, but he managed through the afternoon classes.

When Simon passed the teacher's desk on the way out of the classroom, Mr. Kelly asked, "How do you feel, Simon? You don't look so good. Maybe you'd better go home and rest."

"I'm okay I guess," he responded. Once outside, he forgot all about feeling sick.

On the way home from school Gil, one of his friends, fell into step beside him, "Hey, Simon, we made some really good dams down by the lake yesterday. Let's go and build some more."

Side by side they headed for the shallow lake. Many little streams of runoff from higher ground would travel out on the ice and disappear through it. The snow hadn't completely melted yet so it was great fun making dams across these little streams with the easily packed snow. Simon and Gil finished one large dam, but the water broke through it and cascaded out on the lake ice.

"Come on, Gil, let's build another dam out on the lake," Simon called as he headed out on the ice.

Gil shouted a warning after him, "We'd better not. That ice is pretty rotten out there now. It's thawing out." But it was too late. Simon felt the ice bending and cracking beneath him. He looked vainly around for something to hang onto. There was nothing but slippery ice. Simon clutched the ice at the edge of the hole, but his fingers slipped off. He felt himself sinking.

"Help," he screamed, "Help me!"

Simon felt the cold water enter his boots, then slowly penetrate his clothing.

It was so cold it took his breath away! He screamed again, "Help!"

Standing on the bank, Gil was petrified. He couldn't speak or even move. All he could see was Simon's head above the ice. If he went out on the ice he might fall in too. What should he do?

Suddenly Simon felt his feet touch the muddy bottom. "I'm on the bottom now. It's soft, and I can't stand up. It's cold. Get help!" he yelled through chattering teeth.

Frightened by Simon's screams, Gil ran to the nearest cabin, burst through the door and yelled, "Simon fell through the ice down at the lake! He's drowning!"

Startled, Tony and Billy sprang into action. Leaving their coffee cups, they rushed out of the house, grabbed a coil of rope from a nearby boat and ran down to the lake's edge. They could see Simon's head bobbing above the ice. While Tony held the end of the long rope on the shore, Billy edged his way out on the ice toward the boy.

Simon saw Billy move out on the ice with the rope. The water was so cold he didn't know if he could move. He couldn't feel his feet anymore. He wanted them to hurry.

As soon as he was close enough Billy tied a loop in the rope and threw it to Simon. "Now, put the loop over your head and under your arms and I'll pull you out," he called.

Simon grabbed for the rope but his hands were so numb he couldn't hold on to it.

"It's okay," Billy's voice was calm. "Let's try again."

This time Simon was able to grab the rope. He pulled it over his head, and reached his arms up through it. He tried to grip the rope with his numb fingers. "I don't know if I can hang on."

"Just do your best. I'm gonna start pulling," Billy encouraged as he backed toward shore.

Simon felt himself being raised in the water as the rope tightened around his back. The ice in front crackled as he was thrust forward against it. He tried to hang on but the rope kept slipping out of his numb hands. He looked desperately toward the two men.

Working together, Tony and Billy heaved on the rope and Simon slowly slid up onto the fragile ice. He struggled to stand, but Billy warned, "Don't try to get up yet. You might break through," He stayed limp as the two men dragged him across the ice to shore.

Once he was on firm ground Simon tried to stand, but he couldn't. He had no feeling in his arms or legs. Water dripped from his clothing and his boots were filled with the icy liquid. All color had drained from his face and his lips were blue. He started to shake all over.

"Man that was a close call! Here, I'll carry you up to the house so you can get warm," Tony said as he scooped up the shivering boy and carried him into the house.

Once inside they stripped off Simon's wet clothes and vigorously rubbed him with towels. Then they wrapped him in a blanket and sat him in a chair next to the warm stove. Simon's teeth were chattering uncontrollably as he tried to get warm.

"Here, drink some tea. It'll warm you from the inside," Billy said as he handed Simon a mug. Wrapping both hands around the cup, Simon tried to keep from shaking as he drank the hot tea.

Noticing Gil hovering by the door, Billy commanded, "Gil, you go get Simon's dad. He needs to get this boy home to bed so he can warm up." Gil took off running, letting the door bang behind him.

A short time later Simon's father burst into the room. "What happened? I heard you almost drowned."

Simon looked weakly at his father as Tony said, "You're lucky to have this boy alive. He fell through the ice down at the lake."

Edwin gave his son a long look. "What were you doing down on the lake? I told you not to play on that ice anymore. It's no good."

Simon looked down, then reached up to brush back the lock of hair that had fallen across his face.

Edwin turned to the men, "Boy, I sure wanna thank you fellas for saving my boy. If it weren't for you he'd be out there under the water." He turned back to Simon, "Come on, let's get you home and into some dry clothes."

Simon's father carefully wrapped the blankets around him and carried him all the way home. Even though Simon hadn't been carried like that since he was small, his father's strong arms around him felt good. He was glad to be safe.

Once inside their house his father helped him into dry clothes and put him into bed. His mother filled a mug with hot soup and brought it to him. She watched him as he finished it, then said, "You try to warm up in bed now."

Sleep came easily that evening for Simon, but early the next morning he awoke with sharp pains in his chest. "Mom, Mom, my chest hurts when I try to breathe."

His mother struggled out of bed and came over to him. "What's the matter?" she asked.

"My chest hurts. It's just like somebody's standing on it and I can't breathe good."

"Here, take this aspirin and I'll go get the health aide."

Simon took the aspirin and drifted back to sleep.

The next thing he knew the health aide, a villager who was trained to give medical care, was bending over him, her cool hand on his forehead. "Just lay still, Simon," she said. "Let's take your temperature and I want to listen to your chest."

She took Simon's temperature and looked him over carefully. "His temperature is 103 degrees," Simon heard her tell his mother. Then she turned back to Simon and asked, "How long have you felt this way?"

"I dunno, just today. No, last night I didn't feel so good either. Yeah, maybe a couple of days, and remember, I fell in the lake."

The health aide used her stethoscope to listen to Simon's chest, then said, "Well, your mom will give you some more aspirin in a couple of hours and we'll see how you are doing. I'm going to go over to the clinic and talk to the doctor on the radio about you."

The health aide had a daily radio schedule with the hospital 150 miles away. She would talk with the doctors there about patients' symptoms and they would prescribe medicines the health aide had in the clinic. Extreme cases were sent to the hospital by plane.

By the next morning Simon was no better. "Mom, my chest hurts. I ache all over. I can't take a big breath. What's wrong with me?"

"I dunno, Simon, but I'll get the health aide again. Here, can you drink some of this tea?" his mother said as she held a mug for him to drink. He drank some of the tea and then pushed it away and lay back down.

After the health aide examined him this time, she held a hurried conference with his parents. Simon heard the concern in his dad's voice as he asked,

"What's the matter with him?"

"Well, I talked to the doctor at the hospital and we think he's got pneumonia. His lungs are congested and now his temperature is up to 104."

"Can you give him anything for it?"

"He needs penicillin but I don't have any more. We've had a lot of people sick lately and I used it all up. Some should come in on the mail plane. I ordered it, but the plane's not due until next week."

"There's none in the village?" Edwin asked.

"What should we do?" Simon's mother inquired as she saw the health aide shake her head.

"Well, if he were my boy I'd send him to the hospital as soon as they can get a plane in here. You know pneumonia works fast and his temperature is going up."

Simon's parents knew how dangerous pneumonia could be. Long ago it was common for people to get pneumonia, measles, or the flu and die because there was no medicine or hospital care available to them.

The health aide added, "You know, the mail plane won't come 'til next week. That's too long. Maybe we'd better radio out for a charter plane right away. Do you have enough money to pay for a plane trip to the hospital?"

Simon's dad barely hesitated, "I think so, but do you think the government might pay for it?"

"Usually they do, especially if it's an emergency, but you should have the money just in case. Let's go down and see if we can get a plane in here as soon as possible."

When she heard of Simon's illness, the postmistress radioed a message for a charter plane to come to the village from Tanana, where the hospital was located. Luckily conditions were good for radio transmission and a charter flight was arranged. A plane would leave immediately to take Simon to the hospital.

When they got back to the house Simon's temperature had climbed and he was soaked with sweat.

His mother and father paced the floor nervously waiting for the sound of an airplane.

Just then the health aide re-entered the house. "I've got some bad news. The plane can't come. There's a storm moving in and the pilot doesn't want to risk it."

"But what'll we do now?" Simon's mother asked anxiously.

"We'll just have to hope and pray the weather clears soon. I'm gonna go look at my medicines again and I'll talk to the doctor." She glanced at her watch. "He could have some more aspirin now and make sure he drinks plenty of water."

Simon was vaguely aware of what was going on around him as he drifted in and out of sleep. He remembered seeing Gil peering at him anxiously at his bedside and hearing Gil's voice, unusually quiet, ask, "How are you doing?"

Weakly Simon answered, "I dunno. The plane's supposed to get me, but it can't come."

"I know," Gil replied nervously, "Everybody's praying for you and for that plane to get in."

"Thanks," Simon's reply was weak, and then he slipped back to sleep.

The sound of the airplane roaring over the village woke Simon. "Airplane!" his father shouted. "We'll get you out now!"

Simon let them put him into a sleeping bag with all his clothes on. Weakly he mumbled, "What's going on?"

His father's voice was reassuring. "There was a break in the weather so the plane could come. We'll get you to the hospital now. You just lay still. We'll take care of everything."

Simon drifted into sleep again. The next thing he knew he felt himself bumping along in a sled pulled by a snow machine to the airstrip. He was placed on the floor in the back of the plane whose engine was still running.

"You take it easy with that boy," Simon's dad said. "I'll pay whatever it costs."

The pilot nodded, closed the airplane door, taxied down the frozen airfield, turned around, gunned the engine and took off.

People standing at the airstrip watched the plane rise into the air and disappear in the distance. "I sure hope he'll be okay," the health aide said softly. "I called the hospital and they'll be waiting for him at the airport."

CHAPTER 9
THE HOSPITAL

Simon was only vaguely aware of the plane landing, being helped into the waiting ambulance, and the ride to the hospital. When he awoke he felt himself being rolled over. "Where am I?" he wondered. Then he remembered, he was in the hospital. He had made it. The nurse pulled back the sheets, wiped his hip with alcohol, and plunged a needle in.

"Ouch! That hurt."

"Of course it does," the nurse replied in a cheery voice. "But penicillin does its job! We were really worried about you. It's lucky that the plane got in when it did. Your fever was very high. You still have a fever now, but it's coming down. Here, let's see if you can get these pills down." She handed him a glass of water and nodded at the pills she held in a paper container. "Now how about something to eat? Some Jell-O maybe?"

"No, I'm not hungry," Simon shook his head.

"Okay, but drink this juice and finish all that water if you can," she urged.

Simon drank the juice but he felt too weak to finish the water. He rolled over and went back to sleep. The next time he woke up he looked around. It was quiet and it was dark outside. The lights were out. He wondered how long he had been asleep. He reached to touch the place on his hip that was sore. There were lots of bumps there. How many shots had they given him? How long had he been here? He picked up the glass of water from the bedside table and drained it thirstily. He pulled the covers up and drifted back to sleep.

"Simon, wake up!" He opened his eyes to see a nurse with a thermometer in her hand. "Here, open your mouth," she said as she put the thermometer under his tongue. "You've been resting a long time! You know how long?"

Simon shook his head.

"Three days since you got here."

"Three days?" Simon mumbled, the thermometer still in his mouth. It didn't seem like that long.

The nurse pulled the thermometer out and looked at it. "Your temp has come down, almost to normal now. How do you feel?"

"Better, I guess."

"Feel like eating?"

"Maybe," Simon responded, as he struggled upright and looked at the tray of breakfast on the table beside the bed. He smelled the toast and mush and suddenly he was hungry. "Yeah, I think I could eat some."

As the nurse left the room, she called over her shoulder, "If you finish that you can get more too. The doctor will be by to see you soon."

As Simon attacked his breakfast he looked up and saw the doctor smiling at him from the doorway of his room. "Feeling better now?" he asked as he entered the room.

"Yeah, but I sure feel weak." Simon felt shy in the presence of this big, tall man dressed all in white.

"It's no wonder. You've been very sick. What happened?"

"I dunno. I fell through the ice, I guess." Simon whispered.

"You mean you tried to go swimming at this time of year?" Simon heard a smile in the doctor's booming voice, and suddenly his shyness vanished.

"No, I didn't try to, but I did! Man! I've never been so cold in my life."

Laughing, the doctor asked, "Did you know you had pneumonia?"

"No."

"Well you did, and you're mighty lucky to be getting over it so soon. Kids get sick fast, but they usually get well fast too. We'll watch you for the next few days, keep the shots and medicine coming, and see how you do." The doctor rested his foot on the stool beside Simon's bed and leaned closer. "Simon, I hear people in your village hunt bears in the den. You ever do that?"

"Last year I did, but we didn't get anything."

"That sounds dangerous to me. Is it?"

"Yeah, I guess it is, but my dad knows how. He's done it ever since he was my age."

"Did you ever catch a bear?"

"No, but I sure want to. Maybe next year I'll be lucky."

"Well, you'd better concentrate on getting well right now," the doctor said, straightening up and heading towards the door. "Then you can go hunting."

In the next few days Simon had a chance to look around the hospital. He had never been in one before. Everything smelled funny and it was so clean. Almost every day they changed his bed and the sheets weren't even dirty! And the food... well, it was okay, but it was in such tiny portions on the little tray they brought in. It didn't have much taste to it either. He'd rather have some of his mom's moose soup any day.

Except for the doctor and a few nurses, the people working in the hospital were Athabascan Indians like him. The man who mopped the floor in his room every day told him everyone had trained to do their jobs while working in the hospital. Some prepared the food, some took care of the laundry or cleaned floors, while others worked in the office.

Now that he was able to walk around the hospital, Simon saw the patients were also Indian. The United States government maintained and staffed this hospital so the people living in the area would have good medical services at little or no expense to them.

Simon met some other patients in the children's ward. "What's wrong with you?" he was asked.

"Oh, I had pneumonia. Why are you here?" he asked a boy who looked about his own age.

"I had TB, the boy answered. But the doctor says we just about got it licked now. I'll be able to go home pretty soon."

"So where do you live?" Simon asked.

"Up at Bettles."

Simon recognized the name of the village upriver. "How long have you been here?" he asked.

"I don't know. About a month, I guess."

"Man, that's a long time!" Simon exclaimed.

"Yeah, I know. I sure miss home. My parents came down to visit me once," the boy replied in a small voice that made Simon wish he hadn't brought the subject up.

Simon knew tuberculosis had been one of the deadliest diseases to affect Native Alaskans. Before medicines and treatment had been developed, thousands of people had died from it. Today with proper care and medicines, TB could be cured in a short time, especially if it had not progressed too far. Simon felt lucky he only had pneumonia.

On Friday morning, the doctor came into Simon's room. After listening to his chest, he said, "You're doing pretty well. How would you like to go home?"

"Yeah!" Simon responded without hesitation.

"The mail plane leaves tomorrow for your village. Do you want to be on it?"

Simon nodded emphatically, "I sure do!"

"I think you're well enough to go home now, but I want you take it easy for the next two weeks or so. That means you can go to school, but afterwards go straight home. The health aide will check on you at home too. And," the doctor added with a grin, "no more swimming 'til summer! Otherwise you might end up right back here. You understand?"

Simon smiled in agreement. Then he said, "After breakup when school is out we all hunt muskrats. Do you think it would be all right if I did that?"

"When will it start?"

"Not until school's out. After the ice goes out."

"That sounds okay, but remember, don't work too hard, and no more swimming in ice water!"

"Okay," he joined the doctor in laughter.

The next day Simon was taken to the airport where he caught the mail plane back to the village. As the plane circled his town he could see lots of people waiting for him and for their mail. They looked so tiny! Once the plane was on the ground he felt his father's strong arms lifting him down out of the plane.

"Simon," how do you feel?" His father inquired anxiously.

"I feel okay, just a little weak."

"You should feel weak. You had a temperature of 105 degrees and you didn't eat for three days!"

"How did you know?" Simon blinked in surprise.

"Doctor told us on the radio," the health aide's voice chimed in. "I'm sure glad we got you to the hospital in time."

"Me too," agreed Simon.

It seemed to Simon like all the kids in the village followed him into the house. He was especially happy to see Gil and Ralph. It was good to be home! After he had eaten some of his mother's moose stew and a hotcake with butter and jam, Simon felt sleepy

Mom, I think I'll take a nap," he told his mother.

"It's okay, we have your bed all fixed."

Simon sat on the edge of the bed, took off his boots and climbed in. "You kids play out now. Simon wants to sleep," was the last thing he heard.

When Simon opened his eyes, he looked at the clock. It was eight o'clock...in the morning! He had slept all afternoon and all night! His mother was busy preparing pancakes and smelling them made him hungry. He threw the covers back and, sitting on the edge of the bed, pulled on his boots.

"I see the sleepy boy finally woke up," his mother greeted him.

"Yep, I sure slept a long time."

"Yes, but you needed it."

Simon's legs felt shaky as he walked over to the kitchen table and sat down. His father was seated at the table drinking coffee. He said to Simon, "Remember that gun we were going to order for you?"

"Yeah." Simon's heart skipped a beat. He nervously pushed his hair out of his eyes.

"Well I ordered it from Fairbanks a couple of weeks ago and it just came."

"Where is it?" Simon's voice betrayed his excitement.

"Right here." His hunger temporarily forgotten, Simon raced across the room. He took the gun from his father, "My very own twenty-two, and not a single shot either!" He carefully inspected the gun, then drew a bead on an imaginary target. "Bang! One dead muskrat!"

"Simon, come and eat," his mother called.

CHAPTER 10

MUSKRAT HUNTING

Three weeks had passed since Simon had gotten home from the hospital, and it was the middle of May. School was out and "breakup" was just ahead. Simon walked out to the riverbank and looked down at the angry black water churning through open holes in the ice as the river continued to rise. He was feeling almost well again, so he was trapping muskrats. Early in the morning while everything was still frozen he walked about a mile over the hill and down from the village to a small sheltered lake that had lots of muskrat push-ups in it.

A "push-up" is a mound above the ice about a foot in diameter made by a muskrat pushing the roots and vegetation up from the bottom of a lake. It would hollow this out into a little house where it could get air, rest, and eat the vegetation it had collected. The little animals did not stay long in these houses, but used them for stopping off points in the day's search for the roots and stems of water plants they ate during the winter.

Simon located one of the little hump-shaped igloos on the lake ice and carefully took the top off. He knelt down and set a trap, attached the chain to a birch pole he had cut, and placed the trap on weeds just at the entrance to the house. Although it was harder to trap a muskrat than to shoot one, Simon knew a trapped muskrat pelt brought more money than one with a bullet hole in it. Like with beaver, holes in the pelt cost the trapper money.

When he finished setting the trap, he replaced the vegetation over the house. Each time he came to check his traps he would get four or five muskrats, but he knew the ice was getting weaker. Pretty soon it would no longer support him and he didn't want another accident, so he'd need to pick up his traps on his next trip. It just wasn't worth getting wet and taking a chance on losing his new twenty-two.

Simon checked the last trap and was carefully picking his way around the edge of the lake when he saw a furry brown animal emerge from a hole in the ice fifty feet in front of him. Muskrat! He stopped, put a shell in the chamber and slowly brought the gun to his shoulder.

The muskrat stood up on its hind legs to get a better view. Crack! It tumbled over. Simon had shot his first muskrat with his new twenty-two! He hurried over and put the animal into his pack. He had done it! Now he knew he would be able to get more muskrats after breakup.

A few days later Simon awoke one morning to muffled sounds from somewhere outside. The river ice was going out! Without stopping for breakfast, he ran to join his friends at the bluff. With a cracking, heaving, and groaning, the last sign of winter was being pushed out to sea to make room for the new season.

"Looks like we'll be using our boats in a few days," Gary said. "You gonna hunt rats this year?"

"Yep. I want to use my new twenty-two."

In the village men tested their canoes for leaks, painted their riverboats, and tuned their outboard engines in preparation for the coming season. It was late May and, although there was still ice in a few sheltered lakes, and a patch or two of snow could be found under the protective boughs of the spruce trees, soon all signs of winter would be gone. Runoff from the surrounding areas drained into the river. The water rose and over-flowed its banks, connecting many lakes and low lying areas.

As soon as the river was clear of ice, early one morning Simon's family left the village in their skiff, heading down river to their spring camp. In the front of the long river boat were all the supplies they would use for the next couple of weeks: dried moose meat and fish, canned goods, the tent and sleeping bags, an extra outboard motor, extra gas, and a small canoe. As they moved downstream with the current, Edwin had to drive slowly and watch for stumps, logs, and brush floating down the river. The river was so muddy and full of silt he could hardly see beneath the surface.

Two hours had passed by the time Edwin steered the boat up to shore near their spring camp, a place on a bluff near some lakes. After tying the boat, they climbed up the bank and looked at the flooded land.

"Water is sure everywhere now, isn't it?" Simon commented.

"Yeah, but that's good for hunting 'rats," his dad responded. "High water will make it easier to canoe into the lakes."

When they had unloaded the boat, they located their old campsite high on the bank and set up their wall tent, using the old poles they had left standing last year. The white tent was about twelve feet square and tall enough to stand up in. Next they brought in a small wood stove for heat and cooking. As soon as the stove and stove pipe were set up, Edwin stepped back and said, "You women can finish getting things set up here. We men have to go and see where the muskrats are. Come on, Simon."

Simon felt pride at being called a man by his father, and as they walked down to the boat, he asked, "I'll go with you in the canoe?"

"Yes, we'll try it out this time. We want to look around and see how many 'rats are here. Bring your twenty-two and a couple boxes of shells."

Simon eagerly grabbed his gun and stuffed the shells into his pockets. He looked at the canoe as his father lifted it into the water. It was about eight feet long, two feet wide and its ribs were made of birch. They were bent in a half moon shape and placed every foot or so. The keel or bottom board was also made of birch and hand-bent to fit.

Simon knew working with birch took great skill. He had watched his father and other village men bend a piece of good straight-grained birch almost double without breaking it by steaming the wood first, then gradually and carefully using vices to bend it. This technique also was used for snowshoes and sleds, and it was something they had learned from their fathers before them. Over the past few weeks Simon had watched his father cover the canoe with heavy canvas, then paint it with green waterproof paint. His father told him that in the old days they didn't have canvas or paint so they used birch bark and pitch. The canvas lasted longer and didn't leak like the old birch bark did.

"Come on, let's go! You get in the front," Edwin urged as he pushed the canoe into the water.

Simon stepped carefully into the canoe and sat down near the front. Edwin got in, gave a push with his paddle and they were off. "Now don't make any quick movement like standing up or jumping around or you could have us swimming."

They moved quietly into the first lake. Simon was impressed with the way the small canoe shot forward with each thrust of his father's paddle. He was also proud to be hunting with his father. This was the first year he had come out in the canoe with him.

"Look at that," Edwin said in a hushed voice. "There's two, right there. Go ahead and shoot."

Sure enough, Simon saw two muskrats swimming about twenty-five feet from the canoe. He threw his gun to his shoulder, put a shell in the chamber and fired. Both animals immediately dove.

"You shot too fast." His father said.

Simon nodded, disappointed. There was nothing on the surface now. Where the muskrats would surface next, was anyone's guess.

"Next time, take your time, aim at the head and squeeze off your shot," his father said quietly.

"Okay," Simon nodded.

Simon looked up at the ducks and geese flying close together in pairs as they looked for places to build their nests. Songbirds chirped as they too searched for places to raise their young. It was spring and the land was alive with activity.

Simon glanced up at a nearby tree. "Dad, there's a raven up there watching us. You suppose he'll bring us good luck?"

"I dunno," Edwin replied.

They hadn't gone fifty yards when another muskrat's head bobbed to the surface. Carefully Simon put the gun to his shoulder, pushed off the safety, and squeezed the trigger. Bang!

"You got him! Good shot!" Simon could hear the pride in his father's voice.

"Maybe the raven did help me!" Simon whispered.

They paddled over to the muskrat. Simon reached out, picked it up, and put it on the floor of the canoe behind him. All afternoon they hunted this way. As time passed Simon's shooting steadily improved. He was getting an animal with almost every shot.

Finally his father said, "Well, I think we better head for camp now. I'm getting hungry. What about you?"

Simon had forgotten his hunger while he concentrated on the muskrats. "Yeah, me too. You want to trade places before we go home?"

"You want to try paddling?"

"Okay. And you can try out my twenty-two."

"I'll pull over to shore and we'll trade places."

After they traded places Simon noticed the canoe rode much lower in the bow now that his father was near the front. Controlling the canoe was not easy.

"Just one paddle at a time, and don't push hard. We'll just go slow. And remember, no quick movements," his father cautioned.

"There's one," Simon said softly.

The gun came up and went off in one fluid motion. "Good shot, dad."

"I sure like your gun, Simon, it shoots right where you aim."

Simon agreed with a grin, "Yeah, when you aim it right." He could see his dad smile and nod.

On the way home, Edwin shot five more muskrats. One of the shots was a "double" — two quick shots and two hits. Simon wondered if he ever would be as good a shot as his father.

When they got back and lifted the canoe out of the water, Simon was surprised at the number of muskrats piled inside. His mouth watered at the smell of moose stew his mother had prepared, and he could see she had made frying-pan biscuits too. Simon helped himself to a big bowl of stew, slathered butter on a hot biscuit, sat down cross-legged on the floor of the tent and began to eat.

"Tomorrow I'll cook muskrat for you. Muskrat hunters need to eat muskrat meat to give them good luck," his mother said. Simon liked muskrat meat, especially at this time of year.

"Mom, you know how many 'rats they got?" Rosie asked, her dark eyes dancing with excitement. Before her mother could answer, the words tumbled out, "Thirty-three!"

"My, that's pretty good for the first time out. Who shot them?"

"Simon did," Edwin answered. "With a little more practice he's going to be a good shot."

Though Simon's mouth was stuffed, he nodded vigorously.

After dinner Edwin went out to hunt alone while Simon, his mother and sisters prepared to skin and stretch the skins. As he worked on skinning Simon noticed tiny white things on the muskrat.

"Mom, what are those little white things on the fur?"

"Those are little bugs. Be sure to wash them off when you finish or they'll make you itch."

At that suggestion Simon's arms began to itch, and the more he thought about it the more they itched. Rosie and Sonja began to tease, pointing and pretending they saw more fleas. The tent was filled with their giggles and Simon's protests. His mother smiled and said, "You go ahead and wash up now. I'll finish these. Besides, there's only a few left." Simon gladly stopped. He'd shoot them all right, but skinning was another matter.

When the muskrats were all skinned and the bullet holes sewed shut, Simon's mother and sisters put them on metal and wooden stretchers they had brought. After a day the hides would be dry enough to be taken off the stretchers, and they would keep until it was time to send them off to the buyer.

Simon and his father went muskrat hunting every evening and spent most of the night out. It was the best time to hunt since it was light all night long and the muskrats were out. Night after night they went out. Seldom did they get fewer than a hundred muskrats in a night. Steadily their pile of skins mounted. Each morning Simon fell exhausted into his sleeping bag, but by noon he was ready to hunt some more.

As the days passed there were fewer and fewer muskrats, and several of the ones they had gotten had tears in their skins from fighting. The muskrat's breeding season was coming to an end and the animals were spreading out. Simon's mother would use the torn skins to make hats and mitten linings. Other good skins would be used to make the beautiful fur parkas many villagers wore during the winter, but the best ones would be sold.

The next morning Edwin remarked, "Well I guess we better break camp and get back to town to sell our skins. You know if we get our skins in first they'll get top price."

"Aw, Daddy, can't we stay just a few more days?" begged Rosie.

"We're making a tree house and we don't want to leave yet," Sonja joined in.

"Not this time. Later we'll come down here to fish for our dogs, but now we have to get our skins out."

When the skiff was packed they pushed off from the bank and Simon looked wistfully over his shoulder at their campsite. The days had passed so quickly there had hardly been time for him to get settled in camp.

Now the season was over. On the way back to town he noticed how the river had fallen. Now the banks were visible everywhere and fewer logs floated in the river. The buds on the trees had burst and the first pale green leaves were beginning to show. It was summer!

Once they were back in the village, Simon and his father carried their gunnysacks of muskrat skins to the post office.

"How many 'rats did you get this time, Edwin?" the postmistress asked.

"Maybe about a thousand. Simon here got most of them."

"That's the most I've seen so far. The skins will go out on the next plane. They tell me that a good 'rat skin could bring a dollar and a half this year."

"Good, we can use the money."

When they left the post office, Edwin was thinking about the things they needed that money would buy, but Simon's mind was on other things. I wonder how many rats Gil and Ralph got? If they're back from hunting maybe we can play down at the sand bank. He turned to his father, "I'm gonna go find Gil and Ralph."

CHAPTER 11
THE SNO-GO

Several weeks later as Simon was eating breakfast his dad laid an envelope on the table and said, "Simon, you know how much we got for our rat skins?"

Simon waited, holding his breath, then ventured a soft, "How much?"

"Thirteen hundred and twenty-five dollars!"

Simon's eyes lit up, "Boy! That's a lot! What will we do with it all?"

"Well, you know we need some things like food and traps and gas, but that shouldn't take all of it. We should have several hundred left. What do you think we should get with it?"

"I dunno," Simon answered, but underneath the table he crossed his fingers.

"What do you think about getting a sno-go?"

"Yeah!" Simon burst out, nodding his head vigorously.

His father went on, "I've been thinking, if we had a sno-go, I'd be able to go farther, faster, and catch more in my traps than when I use dogs. That way the machine could pay for itself."

At the mention of their dogs, Simon's heart stopped. "Yeah, but what about our dogs?" Since he helped take care of them, the dogs were his friends. He couldn't bear getting rid of them. He held his breath.

"Oh, no, we won't get rid of them. We'll use them in case the snow-go breaks down. Unless you don't want them anymore...."

"I do, I do," Simon interrupted. "Besides, I like to drive dogs and I want to beat Gary in that race."

"That's right, I forgot about the race. So you want to beat Gary?"

Simon ducked his head and brushed his hair out of his eyes. "Yeah."

"Well, we'll kind of figure on getting a sno-go next fall, but we'll have to wait until then to see how much money we have left. We might not have enough money."

The rest of the summer flew by for Simon. He went back down to the fish camp with his family where they caught and dried fish to feed the dogs during the long winter. He swam in the river shallows with his sisters and played in the sand on the long river bars. He made a bow and arrow to shoot fish and ducks with, but he didn't get any.

He slid down the steep sand banks and filled his shoes, clothes and hair with the fine sand. He hunted for baby bank swallows by reaching into their nests on the steep banks while mother and father swallows hovered around his head. He went for rides on the river with his father to look for ducks and geese, and to check their gill nets for fish to feed their dogs and themselves.

It seemed to Simon the summer was ending too soon. The days got shorter, the weather cooled, and school started again. School was fun at first, but after awhile Simon wished he could be hunting ducks, geese, and moose with his father. One afternoon after a long school day he said, "Dad, can I quit school? I want to go hunting and trapping and all that stuff with you. I can't do that if I'm always in school."

Simon was startled at his father's response.

"Quit school? Don't be crazy! When I was your age they didn't have schools around here and I <u>wanted</u> to learn how to read and write, but I couldn't. I went to school for about a year and I finally taught myself to read, but it was hard and I can't even read as good as you can now. You might not live around here all the time and you've got to make enough to support a family. If you can't read and do math, you might not even be able to get a job. Right now, maybe you could, but when you're grown up everyone else will be better than you, and you'll be left behind. Besides, state law says you have to go until you're sixteen. Don't ask me stupid questions like that again!"

Surprised at the intensity of his father's response, Simon looked down. After a minute he looked up and brushed his dark hair out of his eyes. "But how will I learn to trap and hunt if I have to go to school all the time?"

"We'll do just like we did last year. You can go out weekends with me." With a smile, he added, "Besides if we get a sno-go we'll be able to go further and get back faster."

"I forgot about the sno-go. That would be great!"

"I've been meaning to talk to you about that. It cost us more to get the things we need, so I don't think we have enough money to buy a sno-go this year."

Simon's heart sank. "We won't be able to get one?"

"Not unless we can get some money from another place."

"But where would we get the money?" Simon asked hopefully.

"Well, I've been thinking. You know how dog racers always come here to buy good dogs for the sled dog championship races in Fairbanks and Anchorage?"

"Yes, but we've never sold our dogs to them." Suddenly Simon was worried.

"That's right, because we needed them. But now if we want a sno-go we might have to sell some."

"You wouldn't sell Queenie and Prince, our leaders, would you?" Simon asked anxiously.

"No, they're our best dogs, but how about a couple of the others?"

"Who would want to buy them?"

"I'm not sure, but those guys always ask about our dogs when they come here. We could write and ask."

"How much do you think they would pay us for good dogs?"

"Maybe five hundred for dogs and a couple hundred for year-old pups."

"Dad, we won't sell our really good dogs, will we? We need to keep our main team...but I'd sure like to have a sno-go too."

"We'll see. I'll write those guys in Fairbanks and Anchorage and see if anyone is interested.

A few weeks passed, then Edwin received a letter from Bill Stuart, a well-known Anchorage dog musher. He said he was coming to look over the dogs for himself and would be in on the next mail plane.

While Simon really wanted a sno-go, he began to worry about losing their dogs. He followed his dad and

Bill home from the mail plane and curled up on a chair in the corner, hoping to hear everything they said.

After Bill was settled at their kitchen table with a cup of coffee, the first question he asked Edwin was why he wanted to sell dogs. He wondered what had changed his mind.

"You remember how many times before I've asked you to sell me some of your dogs? What about that blue-eyed leader I wanted to buy about five years ago? I offered you a thousand dollars for him and you turned me down."

"Blue was a good lead dog, but I needed him for my team. This year we want to buy a sno-go and we don't have enough money, so we'll sell a couple of our dogs."

"Oh, so you want an 'iron dog,'" Bill said smiling.

"Yes, but we'll still keep our main team. Dogs don't break down."

Satisfied, Bill finished his coffee, then stood. "Well, let's have a look at the dogs."

They walked out to the dog yard. Bill carefully examined each dog he was shown. Simon hovered nearby, worrying about which dogs he might want.

As he watched Bill examine the dogs he couldn't help asking, "What are you looking for?"

"Well, young fella. I check for age, have a look at their teeth, the depth of their bodies, see how long the legs are, and feel their coats. Race dogs have to be in really good health so they can run for long distances without tiring. Looks like you have some good dogs here. I think I could use a couple of them in my team right now."

Simon, his father, and Bill stood by the cabin overlooking the dog yard. Simon pushed his hair out of his eyes and looked from one to the other.

Finally Bill spoke, "Well, Edwin, how many do you think you want to sell?"

"That depends on how many you want and how much you'll give me for them."

Simon closed his eyes and wished Bill wouldn't ask for Queenie, Prince, or even Blue.

Pointing at different dogs, Bill said, "I'll give you two hundred apiece for those three pups and five hundred for that spotted dog, unless you want to sell me more."

Edwin looked around his dog yard, "No, I think that's enough for this time."

Simon's breathed a sigh of relief. Queenie and Prince were safe! He quickly added the numbers in his head. Eleven hundred dollars for four dogs, three of them so young they hadn't proven themselves yet. He sucked in his breath. Maybe dog raising paid better than trapping!

"Let's see, a Polaris sno-go costs about a thousand, and it'll be around another hundred for the freight to get it here. Do you want me to write you a check or would you rather I just picked up a sno-go and sent it to you when I get back to Anchorage?" Bill asked.

"Yeah, you could probably get a better price down there than I could from here. Sounds like a good deal to me," Edwin agreed.

They shook hands. Bill would buy the snow machine for Edwin and send him any money that was left. In turn he would take the dogs with him.

Simon buried his face in Queenie's fur and gave Prince's head an affectionate rub, glad that his old friends weren't leaving. "Don't worry. We're never gonna get rid of you guys. You belong here!"

*   *   *

Each time Simon heard the familiar call, "Mail plane!" he wondered if this would be the day. He watched through the school window as the group of villagers streamed to the landing strip. Will our snow-go be on this one? What if that guy forgets, or doesn't keep his word?

Finally, after two long weeks had passed a shiny new Polaris snow machine was unloaded from the mail plane and trucked to their house.

After mail was distributed everyone went up to Edwin's to see the new snow machine. When the skis were attached, the windshield put on, and the gas line connected, Edwin filled the tank and started the engine. A broad smile was on his face. There was no snow yet, but a little trial on bare ground wouldn't hurt.

Simon ran all the way home from school. When he saw the snow machine sitting in front of the house he begged his dad for a ride. Although they went only a short distance on the snowless ground, Simon could hardly believe the power the machine had. This sno-go wouldn't get tired and slow down coming home like the dogs did!

Simon could hardly wait for trapping and bear hunting seasons. He would be setting his own traps and would help shoot a moose and look for bears. He would be driving dogs by himself. And maybe, just maybe, if he acted grown-up enough, his dad might let him drive the new sno-go!

The days grew shorter, the weather cooled, birch leaves turned golden and fell to the ground. Bear season was approaching. Would they use the new machine to go after bears? Simon wasn't sure. The sno-go might scare the bears and bring them bad luck again. What would his father think?

CHAPTER 12

THE BEAR HUNT

Saturday finally arrived. The ground was frozen and it was covered with a light snow. It was time to look for bears. At breakfast Simon asked his father, "We'll take the sno-go?"

Edwin hesitated, then replied, "No, we better keep with the old ways. Dogs are quiet and we want to do things right. We'll take seven dogs. Ground is pretty rough out there now, we don't wanna go too fast."

Simon finished his breakfast and went out to get the traces ready for hitching up the dogs. Would they have good luck this time? Or would the dens be empty, like before. Simon brushed the dark hair from his forehead and finished packing the sled.

As Edwin came out of the cabin, Simon said, "I think I 'bout got everything ready. All we need to do is hitch up the dogs. It's plenty light now. Where will we go this time?"

"We'll go back down to that same birch hill where we hunted before. That's a good place. Bears like it around there," Edwin replied.

Heedless of the bumps on the trail, Simon's mind raced ahead. Would they find any new dens? Would there be a bear in one? Before long Simon heard his father speak to the dogs and felt the sled come to a halt. He jumped out and helped chain the dogs.

As they pushed their way through the brush, Simon glanced up and saw a raven just above the trees, flying the same direction they were walking. Was this a good sign? He hurried to catch up with his father.

"We'll try that same den we looked at last year. It's in a good spot," Edwin said quietly as he continued up the hill. Suddenly he stopped and pointed. "There it is."

Simon pushed his way forward, "Is there one in there?"

"Maybe," his dad answered with a grin.

Simon found the entrance to the den, an oblong hole about two feet high and a foot across, leading down at a rather steep angle into blackness. He noticed a mat of grass in the entrance as a sort of doorway. His father pulled out the grass and pressed a thin, six-foot-long green willow stick he had cut into Simon's hands. Gingerly, Simon pushed the stick down into the den. Finally after most of the stick disappeared, he hit something. It felt funny so he dropped the stick and watched it. It moved slowly up and down. A bear was in there!

Simon nervously pushed his hair out of his eyes. "What do we do now?" he whispered. Then, without giving his father a chance to answer, he asked, "How do we know he won't come out after us?"

"Just listen to him," his dad answered. "He's sound asleep." Dropping to his hands and knees, Simon carefully lowered his head to the entrance of the den and listened. He heard the sound of heavy muffled breathing. Leaning close to the den's entrance, Edwin spoke to the sleeping bear in the Koyukon language, saying, "Go easy, Mr. Bear. We are your friends. We need your meat and we will do everything in the right way, for we respect you."

"Why did you say that?" Simon asked softly.

"Because we respect the bear. He has a powerful spirit. If we don't do it that way we could have bad luck. You don't want bad luck do you?"

Simon shook his head. "No, I want to be a good hunter, just like you."

"Then you have to respect the animals you hunt and remember the old ways. That's how we do it."

After cutting two long birch poles about three inches thick, they roped them together across the den entrance in an X formation, then tied them in place to nearby trees. This was to protect them in case the bear did wake up and try to get out of the den. Simon had heard stories about bear hunters too eager to remember the old ways who had been injured by escaping bears.

Next Edwin used his ax to chop a small hole in the frozen ground through the roof of the den. After about eight inches of earth had been chopped away the ax head pierced the den. They listened carefully. Just snoring. The bear was still asleep. Quietly they enlarged the hole and then took turns peering down into the blackness. They could see nothing.

"Throw a little snow in there."

The snow landed on the bear's fur and now Simon could just make out its shape.

"Since this is your hunt, you'll have to shoot him. Here, take my rifle."

His father handed him the gun and pointed where to shoot. Simon could feel his heart pounding. He took a deep breath, put a shell into the chamber, pushed off the safety, then hesitated. He looked up at his dad, then back into the hole. This was it. This was what he had waited so long for. He thrust the gun to within inches of the bear, and pulled the trigger.

Boom! Knocked back by the kick of the gun and surprised by all the dust that arose as a result of the shot, Simon blinked hard, and then leaned down to look in the den.

"Better shoot him again. I can still hear him breathing," he heard his father say.

Simon put another shell into the chamber, braced his feet, pushed the gun forward and fired again. Boom! All was quiet. The dust settled and there was only silence.

Edwin gingerly poked the bear several times with the willow stick from the top of the den, but there was no response. "Well, I guess we better get him out."

They untied the poles and removed them from the den entrance. Edwin handed Simon a rope and said, "Here, take this in there and tie it around the bear's neck so we can get him out."

Simon took a deep breath and squirmed into the den. The entrance was small and even for him it was a tight squeeze. What if the bear wasn't dead yet, or what if there were other bears in the den besides the one that he had shot? He knew sometimes young bears denned with their mothers. He couldn't see anything in the blackness so he kept his hands close in front of him to feel where he was going as he inched his way forward. Sand from the walls and ceiling fell into his face and went down his neck.

Then he felt something! It was the bear! Simon held his breath and listened carefully for any other sounds in the den. All he heard was the pounding of his own heart. Hands shaking, he found the bear's head and inched the rope around it's neck and tied it. Then he elbowed his way backward carefully, and finally he was back in the bright sunlight. He blinked his eyes to accustom them to the light, brushed the dirt off his clothes, and handed the other end of the rope to his father. Together they pulled on the rope. Tug as they would, the bear didn't move.

"It must be a big one," Edwin said quietly.

"What do we do now?" Simon asked.

"Get one of those poles over there and we'll move him around a bit."

Using the pole to move the bear, they pulled again, and it slowly emerged from the den.

A huge grin spread across Simon's face as he saw the glossy black animal lying in front of him. "It <u>is</u> a big one!" he exclaimed.

"He is." Edwin agreed, taking his knife from the bag. He carefully slit the bear's eyes. "That's so he won't see you. Now you cut some small birch brush to put the meat on while I take care of it."

Simon used the ax to cut down several small birch trees and laid them on the ground near the bear. Meanwhile Edwin removed the bear's entrails and proceeded to skin it. The thick layer of fat just under the hide showed that the bear was in prime condition. Simon helped his father cut the bear meat into pieces and place it on the poles he had cut. Carefully they laid the bear skin over the meat to keep the ravens away.

"How come we're gonna leave the meat here?" Simon asked.

"Bears have powerful spirits and we have to let things settle down before we take it back. Some parts we won't take back at all."

"Which ones?"

"Mainly the head and the skin. They are the strongest. They stay here. We don't want to make it angry 'cause it could try to get even with us by giving us bad luck. We have to do things the right way."

Simon nodded in understanding. He had heard many stories about bears.

"Now I think we should make a fire and have some tea before we go back." They moved a distance away from the den and Edwin started a fire while Simon went down to a small lake nearby where he chopped through the ice, filled a small bucket with water, and washed his hands. He felt his cheeks stiff from smiling. It had really happened! He had caught his first bear! He wanted to jump and shout, but then he knew his father was waiting for the water, so he hurried back.

By the time he returned his father had gotten out their food. Simon nibbled on smoked salmon while he waited for the water to boil. "We'll cook some of the bear meat?" he asked.

"No, it's too soon. We won't eat it for a few days yet."

They finished their meal, extinguished the fire, gathered their equipment and walked back to the dogs and sled.

"I'll come down tomorrow and get the meat," Edwin assured him.

"Can I come too?"

"You have to go to school."

"Oh yeah, I forgot." Oh well, Simon thought, it was worth a try!

The sled ride home seemed like a dream to Simon. He was bursting with pride. He had shot a bear—a big one too. He must be a real Koyukon man now!

"You think they'll have a bear party pretty soon, Dad?" he asked hopefully.

"Yeah, I think pretty soon."

"We'll give some of my meat to the party?" Simon inquired.

"Uh huh. Remember, it's important to share with others, especially since this is your first bear."

"I remember," he said, thinking of how he could now share his catch the way others had done for generations. His thoughts sped ahead to the celebration. He imagined giving his bear meat to the men in the village and how they might look at him differently.

"Please let the party be soon," he said quietly to himself.

CHAPTER 13

THE BEAR PARTY

The following week seemed like the longest in Simon's life. He could think of nothing but the coming bear party. Finally Sunday afternoon arrived and Simon and his father hooked up their dogs to go to the bear party. In their sled was a large mound of frozen bear meat carefully wrapped in a clean tarp. As they moved out of the village Simon sat excitedly in the back of the sled. His father asked him, "Simon, you remember why we have bear parties?"

"Yeah, so we can eat bear meat and tell stories."

"Well that's right, but there's another reason too. It's important to honor the bear that you got. It's like a funeral for the bear where we try to show how much we appreciate what he has given us. Also it helps us to have good luck in the future. A long time ago we used to have the bear party right by where we got him, but we don't do that now 'cause we live in a village."

"How come women can't go to a bear party?"

"I told you before, it's bad luck for the hunter if women have much to do with bears. Bears have powerful spirits and it could be bad luck for the women <u>and</u> the hunter, so we don't do it. Why do we believe that? I dunno, but it's worked for us for a long time, so we're not gonna change it."

The place for the celebration was a spruce grove about three miles from the village and off the main trail. When Simon and his father pulled up they noticed several men and boys had already arrived and were busy cutting dry wood for the fire. While they were tying up their dogs Chief Henry walked over to Simon and Edwin, and grinning broadly, said:

"I see you brought a lot of meat. That's going to bring you good luck, you know."

Simon, remembering what his father had told him, said, "It's important to share."

Chief Henry looked at Edwin and said, "You're teaching him well. He's gonna be a good hunter." Simon looked down, but his heart soared. They carried the tarp filled with meat over near the large crackling fire.

Simon helped fill the large pots and buckets with water and the men lifted them onto the ends of poles stuck in the ground where they would hang over the fire. Then chunks of bear meat were placed in the pots and everyone waited for them to boil. There were also bear paws for roasting. Simon followed his father's lead and took one of these, impaled it on a stick, and thrust it into the fire. The men nearby wrinkled their noses at the acrid smell of burning hair. When the hair was singed off, they threw the charred paws into the pot with the rest of the boiling meat. It would take time for the meat to cook, but Simon knew the wait would be worth it.

He looked around. Men and boys continued to arrive on snow machines and dog teams, bringing food and pots to cook in. While others were busy gathering wood for the fire Simon's friend, Gil, came over and asked him, "They gonna start telling stories pretty soon?"

"Looks like it," Simon replied, glancing toward the old people sitting on logs near the fire. He edged closer along with the others.

Chief Henry sat down cross-legged in front of the fire. He took out his pipe, filled and lit it. A hush gradually fell over the group. He nodded to Jimmy who cleared his throat and began his tale:

Long ago, where the Kateel and Koyukuk Rivers join up, a man's daughter had been really sick for a long time. The medicine man knew this, and tried to cure her sickness. During her treatment she went to the river for water and didn't return. She had disappeared. People searched for her, but found nothing and figured she had probably drowned.

A few days later, tracks like hers were seen by her father further up the Kateel River on a sand bar. Again he searched, but still found no trace of his daughter.

Later that fall, the village of Koyukuk, way down on the Yukon River, that's more than fifty miles away, began missing dried fish. After that winter nothing more was missing at Koyukuk, but two hundred miles down the Yukon at a village called Holy Cross, dried fish and fish eggs stored in little birch baskets began disappearing from the caches where the people stored their meat. One day a seventeen-year-old boy was walking back to the village when he saw a woodswoman leaving a smokehouse with dried fish.

Now you know that woodsmen and woodswomen are people who live all alone in the woods. We don't know how they got there and why they stay away like that. But we do know that they can bring bad luck. These people believed that if a person sees a woodswoman and tells anybody, they could die.

This worried the boy so much he could not eat or sleep for several days. He began to lose weight and got more afraid as time passed. His sister, who was about his age, knew that something was bothering him, so she took him a ways from the village, built a fire, cooked him some fish and said, 'You will die if you don't eat, so eat and tell me what is bothering you.' After much coaxing he ate some of the fish and told her what he had seen.

The story spread through the village, but the older people were afraid to do anything about it. Then five friends of the boy decided to try to capture the woodswoman. They dug shallow holes in the ground near the cache by the woods. Then in the evening they climbed in and covered themselves with grass. The boy who had seen her was to be the lookout, and he would signal them by whistling when he saw her. As it got dark she finally did come, but when he tried to whistle he was too scared for any sound to come out. One of his friends thought he heard something and peeked out of the grass. As the woodswoman paused, he reached out and grabbed her leg, and began yelling for help. The others came out of their hiding places to help. They got her, but it took all of them to hold her.

When they had her tied up they couldn't decide what to do with her. They finally agreed to carry her back to the village and put her in a small cabin by the river. They piled logs around it to keep her from getting away. At first she wouldn't eat or drink anything. Finally the boy who saw her first brought food to her and she began to eat and drink.

Later on they cut her ropes off and she became more friendly, but she still was kept in the little cabin. She didn't know their language and they didn't know hers. One day they let her out of the cabin and she walked down to the Yukon River holding a small girl by the hand. She had the small girl wash her very carefully, and when she came back she was a "new person." She stayed with the people of Holy Cross and even learned their language.

Chief Henry nodded to Jimmy, leaned back, and puffed on his pipe, signaling the end of the story. Simon was so caught up in the tale he had forgotten about the bear meat.

After a long pause one of the men said, "I guess the meat's about ready now."

And it was. The steaming meat was placed to cool on four-foot long birch logs split especially for this occasion. Old people were served first, but after that it was "everyone for himself." Simon grabbed a large chunk of meat and, holding it in one hand, began cutting off pieces with his knife and popping them into his mouth. Man, was this meat good!

"Simon, don't eat too much fat. Might be bad luck for you!" his uncle Franklin laughed as he passed by. Simon joined in the laughter, but he remembered the last bear party where he and the teacher had both suffered upset stomachs from eating too much bear fat with the meat.

Simon ate the tasty meat and Pilot Bread and washed them down with cups of strong tea. He never remembered feeling so good. The fire became a deeper red. The spruce trees turned from green to dark, and the shadows lengthened. It was time to get home and feed the dogs before dark, but Simon didn't want the day to end. The men started dividing the remaining meat among the families at the party. As Simon looked at their pot full of steaming meat, he turned to his father,

"Dad, I should give this meat to Chief Henry."

"Go ahead, if you want," his father replied.

Simon walked over to where the old man was seated and thrust the full pot of meat towards him. "Here, you should have this."

Chief Henry looked up and his eyes crinkled as he smiled and reached to accept the offering. "So, the bear hunter wants to share what he caught. I remember my first bear. I did that too, and it's been good luck for me. I hope you have good luck too. Things are a lot different now than when I was your age, but you are starting out the right way. Learn the old ways. They will help you in your future no matter what happens."

Simon softly replied with the Koyukon word for thank you, "Baasee."

He watched as the men cleaned up from the party. Bones from the bear were put into the fire to burn. Soon there would be no trace left of the party. As they were hooking up the dog team for the ride back home, Simon overheard one of the men say, "Simon's bear sure tasted good. I hope he gets another one next year." Simon felt warm all over.

On the way home Simon thought to himself, "I must almost be a man now that I've killed a bear and had a bear party. How come I don't feel much different? Everything seems pretty much the same. Before I caught that bear I thought getting a bear would change everything. All year I've thought about this and tried to do things right so I'd have good luck. I've worked hard at following my dad's instructions on hunting and trapping and other things, and I've learned a lot, but there's so much more to learn. I want to be a better dog musher so I can beat Gary. I want to be able to trap all by myself. I'd like to drive our new sno-go. It seems like I'm just starting out and yet things are changing so fast. What will it be like in my future? I want to learn the old ways and the new ways too. Man that's a lot to learn!"

Then he thought about the bear party and Chief Henry's words to him. "Learn the old ways. They will help you in your future no matter what happens."

Simon leaned back in the sled, looked up at the sky, and smiled.

About the Author

Mike Cline taught many years in the Alaskan bush and, for two years, lived in Huslia, the village that inspired *Bear Hunter*. Impressed by the villagers' independence and how their children were taught the "old ways," he wanted to record what things were like.

Mike has written professional and popular articles including several about Huslia: "Huslia's Hole Hunters," "Huslia-Village on the Move," and "Spring and 'the Rat'" which were published in *Alaska Magazine*. "Huslia's Hole Hunters" was included in *The Last Frontier, Incredible Tales of Survival, Exploration, and Adventure from Alaska Magazine* described as "fifty-nine stories representing sixty-seven years of the best writing in Alaska." He is the author of a book: *Tannik School, The Impact of Formal Education on the Eskimos of Anaktuvuk Pass.*

He earned a Ph.D. from the University of Oregon specializing in culture change and its impact on Native Alaskans. Mike and his wife Dotty live and write in Homer, Alaska.

Made in the USA
Charleston, SC
15 May 2010